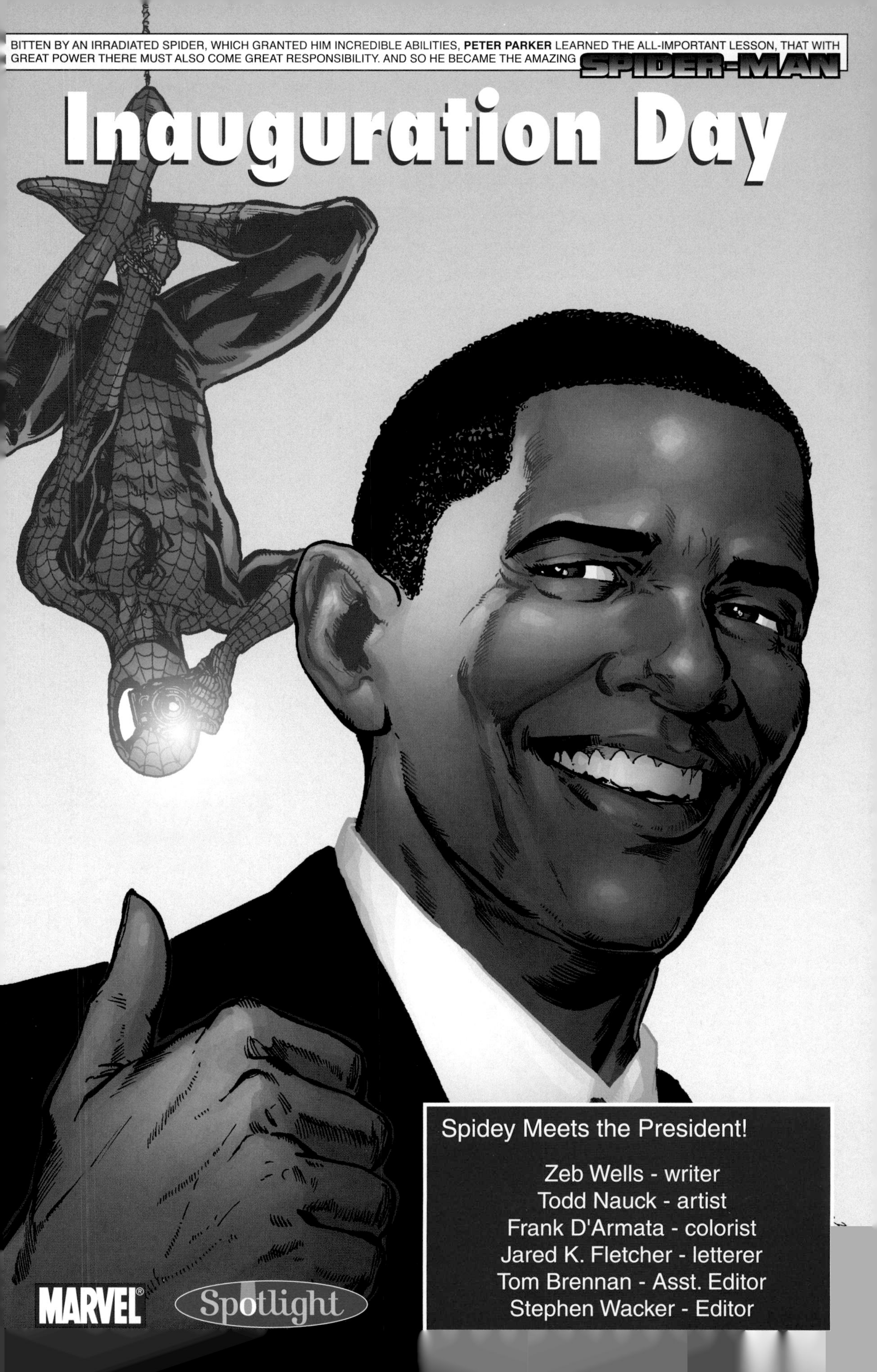
BITTEN BY AN IRRADIATED SPIDER, WHICH GRANTED HIM INCREDIBLE ABILITIES, PETER PARKER LEARNED THE ALL-IMPORTANT LESSON, THAT WITH GREAT POWER THERE MUST ALSO COME GREAT RESPONSIBILITY. AND SO HE BECAME THE AMAZING SPIDER-MAN
Inauguration Day
Spidey Meets the President!
Zeb Wells - writer
Todd Nauck - artist
Frank D'Armata - colorist
Jared K. Fletcher - letterer
Tom Brennan - Asst. Editor
Stephen Wacker - Editor
MARVEL®
Spotlight

VISIT US AT
www.abdopublishing.com

Reinforced library bound edition published in 2011 by Spotlight, a division of the ABDO Group, 8000 West 78th Street, Edina, Minnesota 55439. Spotlight produces high-quality reinforced library bound editions for schools and libraries. Published by agreement with Marvel Characters, Inc.

Printed in the United States of America, Melrose Park, Illinois.
042010
092010
This book contains at least 10% recycled material.

Library of Congress Cataloging-in-Publication Data

Wells, Zeb.
  Inauguration Day / story, Zeb Wells ; art, Todd Nauck. Gettysburg distress! / writer, Matt Fraction ; artist, Andy Macdonald. Fight at the museum / writer, Zeb Wells ; art, Derec Donovan. -- Reinforced library ed.
      p. cm. -- (Spider-Man (Series))
  "Marvel."
  "The Amazing Spider-Man Presidents' Day Special ... A Marvel History-In-The-Making Classic featuring Captain America and Abraham Lincoln!!"--p. 12.
  Summary: Spider-Man has a series of adventures on the day of Barack Obama's inauguration as President of the United States.
  ISBN 978-1-59961-777-0
  1. Graphic novels. [1. Graphic novels. 2. Superheroes--Fiction. 3. Obama, Barack--Inauguration, 2009--Fiction.] I. Nauck, Todd, ill. II. Fraction, Matt. III. Macdonald, Andy, artist, ill. IV. Donovan, Derec, ill. V. Title. VI. Title: Gettysburg distress. VII. Title: Fight at the museum.
  PZ7.7.W45In 2010
  741.5'973--dc22
                                2009052841

All Spotlight books have reinforced library bindings and are manufactured in the United States of America.

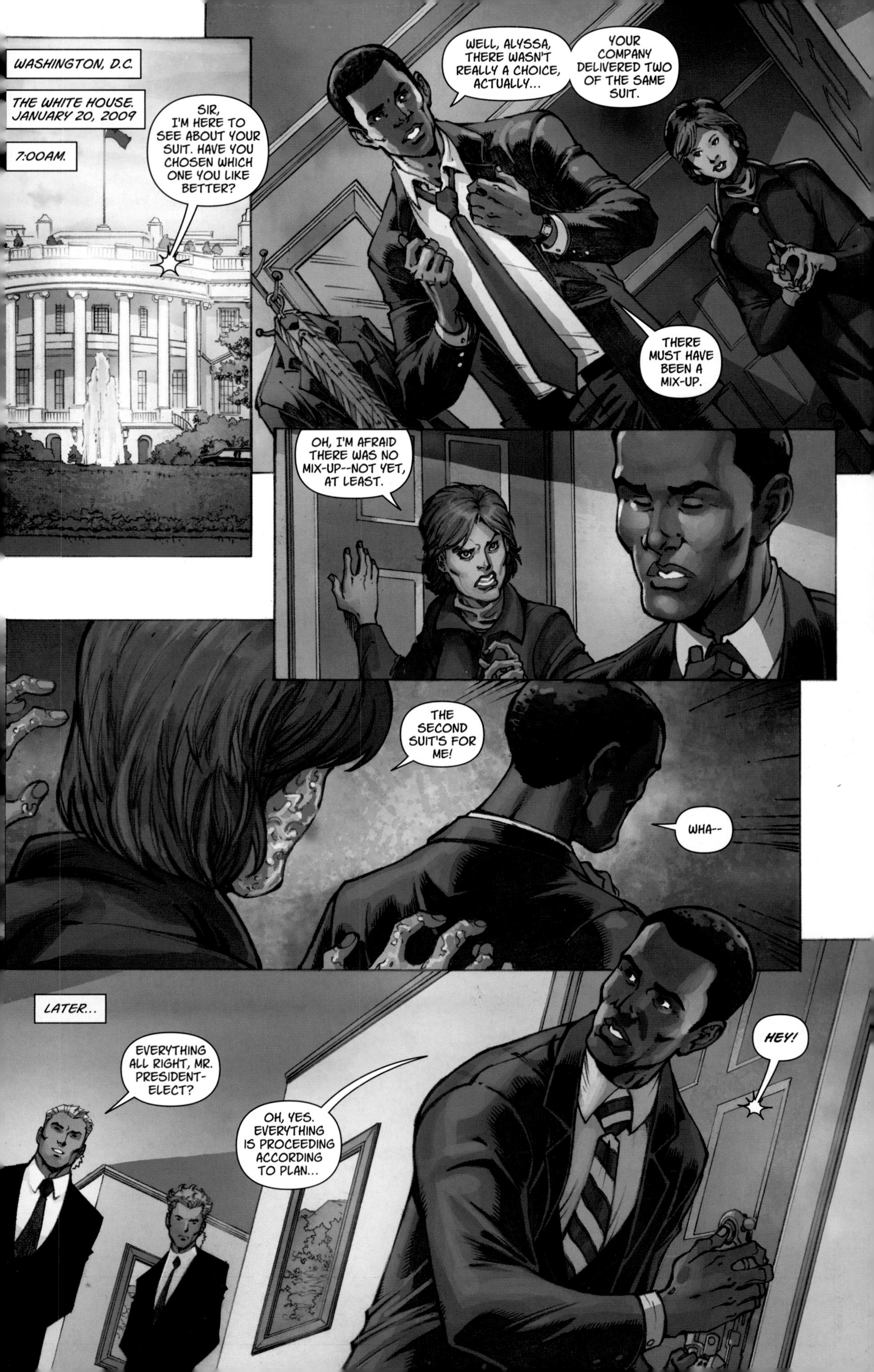
WASHINGTON, D.C.
THE WHITE HOUSE. JANUARY 20, 2009
7:00AM.
SIR, I'M HERE TO SEE ABOUT YOUR SUIT. HAVE YOU CHOSEN WHICH ONE YOU LIKE BETTER?
WELL, ALYSSA, THERE WASN'T REALLY A CHOICE, ACTUALLY...
YOUR COMPANY DELIVERED TWO OF THE SAME SUIT.
THERE MUST HAVE BEEN A MIX-UP.
OH, I'M AFRAID THERE WAS NO MIX-UP--NOT YET, AT LEAST.
THE SECOND SUIT'S FOR ME!
WHA--
LATER...
EVERYTHING ALL RIGHT, MR. PRESIDENT-ELECT?
OH, YES. EVERYTHING IS PROCEEDING ACCORDING TO PLAN...
HEY!

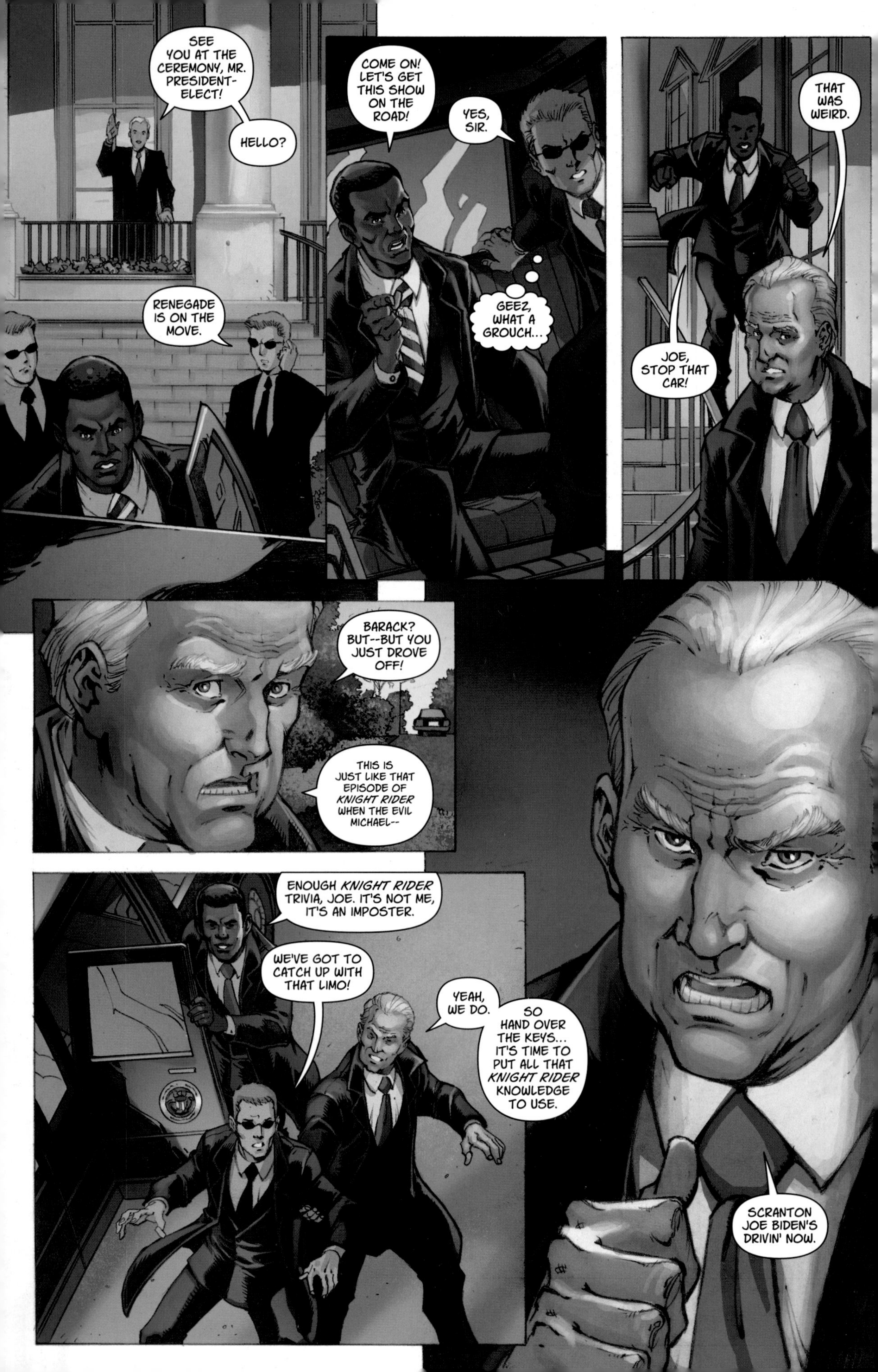
SEE YOU AT THE CEREMONY, MR. PRESIDENT-ELECT!
HELLO?
RENEGADE IS ON THE MOVE.
COME ON! LET'S GET THIS SHOW ON THE ROAD!
YES, SIR.
GEEZ, WHAT A GROUCH...
THAT WAS WEIRD.
JOE, STOP THAT CAR!
BARACK? BUT--BUT YOU JUST DROVE OFF!
THIS IS JUST LIKE THAT EPISODE OF KNIGHT RIDER WHEN THE EVIL MICHAEL--
ENOUGH KNIGHT RIDER TRIVIA, JOE. IT'S NOT ME, IT'S AN IMPOSTER.
WE'VE GOT TO CATCH UP WITH THAT LIMO!
YEAH, WE DO.
SO HAND OVER THE KEYS... IT'S TIME TO PUT ALL THAT KNIGHT RIDER KNOWLEDGE TO USE.
SCRANTON JOE BIDEN'S DRIVIN' NOW.

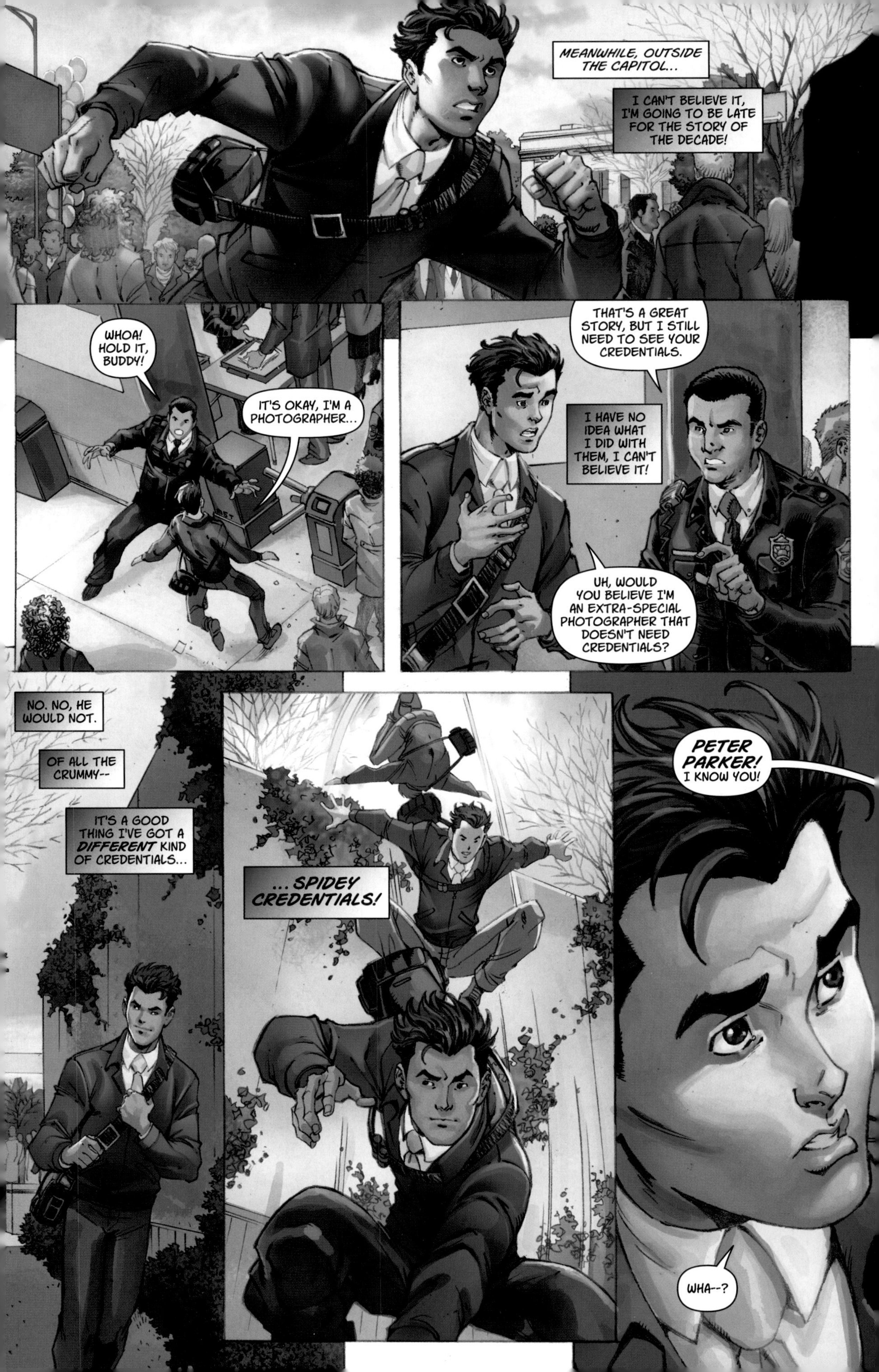
MEANWHILE, OUTSIDE THE CAPITOL...
I CAN'T BELIEVE IT, I'M GOING TO BE LATE FOR THE STORY OF THE DECADE!
WHOA! HOLD IT, BUDDY!
IT'S OKAY, I'M A PHOTOGRAPHER...
THAT'S A GREAT STORY, BUT I STILL NEED TO SEE YOUR CREDENTIALS.
I HAVE NO IDEA WHAT I DID WITH THEM, I CAN'T BELIEVE IT!
UH, WOULD YOU BELIEVE I'M AN EXTRA-SPECIAL PHOTOGRAPHER THAT DOESN'T NEED CREDENTIALS?
NO. NO, HE WOULD NOT.
OF ALL THE CRUMMY--
IT'S A GOOD THING I'VE GOT A *DIFFERENT* KIND OF CREDENTIALS...
...SPIDEY CREDENTIALS!
PETER PARKER! I KNOW YOU!
WHA--?

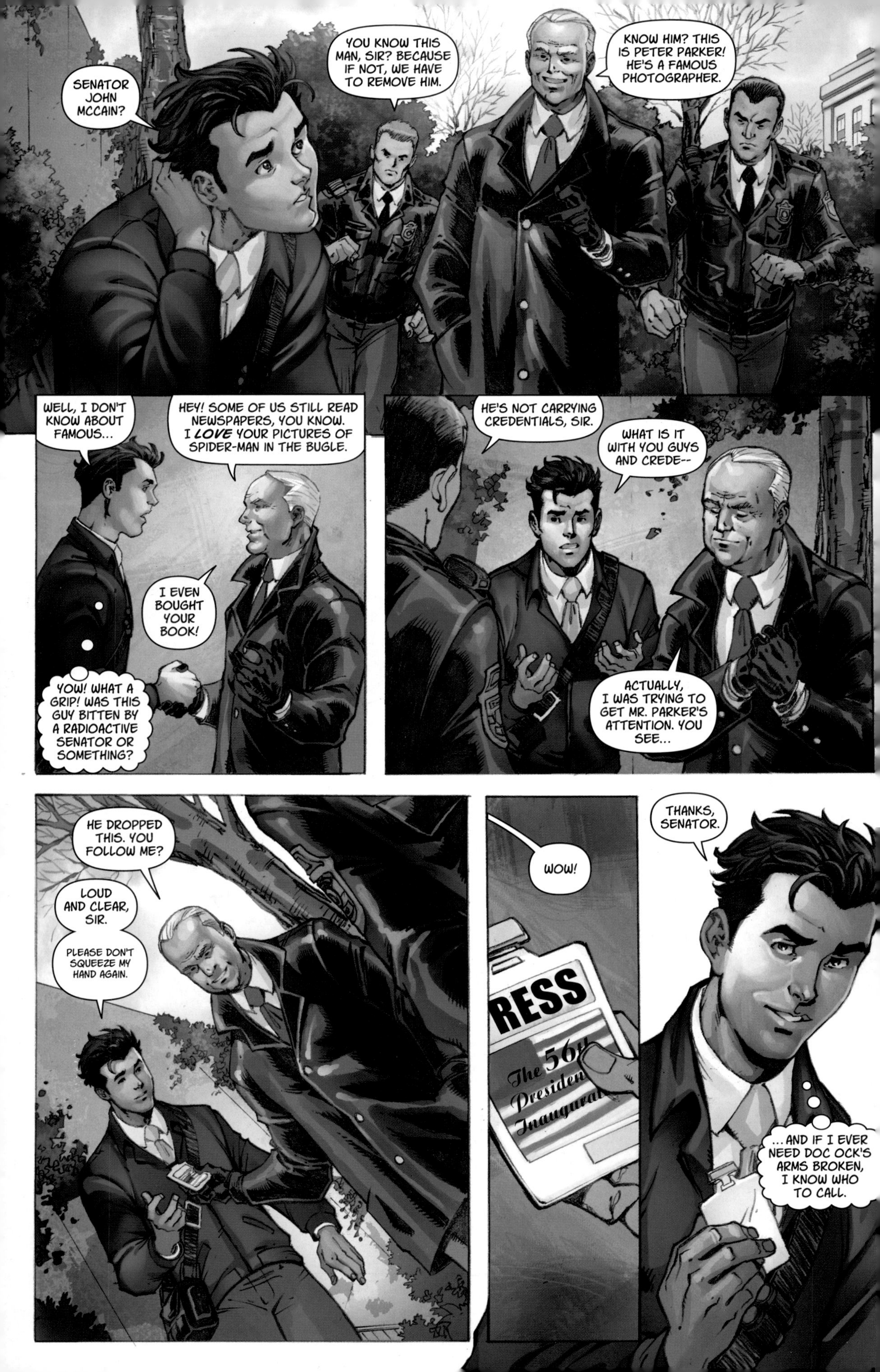
SENATOR JOHN MCCAIN?
YOU KNOW THIS MAN, SIR? BECAUSE IF NOT, WE HAVE TO REMOVE HIM.
KNOW HIM? THIS IS PETER PARKER! HE'S A FAMOUS PHOTOGRAPHER.
WELL, I DON'T KNOW ABOUT FAMOUS...
HEY! SOME OF US STILL READ NEWSPAPERS, YOU KNOW. I LOVE YOUR PICTURES OF SPIDER-MAN IN THE BUGLE.
I EVEN BOUGHT YOUR BOOK!
YOW! WHAT A GRIP! WAS THIS GUY BITTEN BY A RADIOACTIVE SENATOR OR SOMETHING?
HE'S NOT CARRYING CREDENTIALS, SIR.
WHAT IS IT WITH YOU GUYS AND CREDE--
ACTUALLY, I WAS TRYING TO GET MR. PARKER'S ATTENTION. YOU SEE...
HE DROPPED THIS. YOU FOLLOW ME?
LOUD AND CLEAR, SIR.
PLEASE DON'T SQUEEZE MY HAND AGAIN.
WOW!
RESS
The 56th Presiden Inaugura
THANKS, SENATOR.
...AND IF I EVER NEED DOC OCK'S ARMS BROKEN, I KNOW WHO TO CALL.

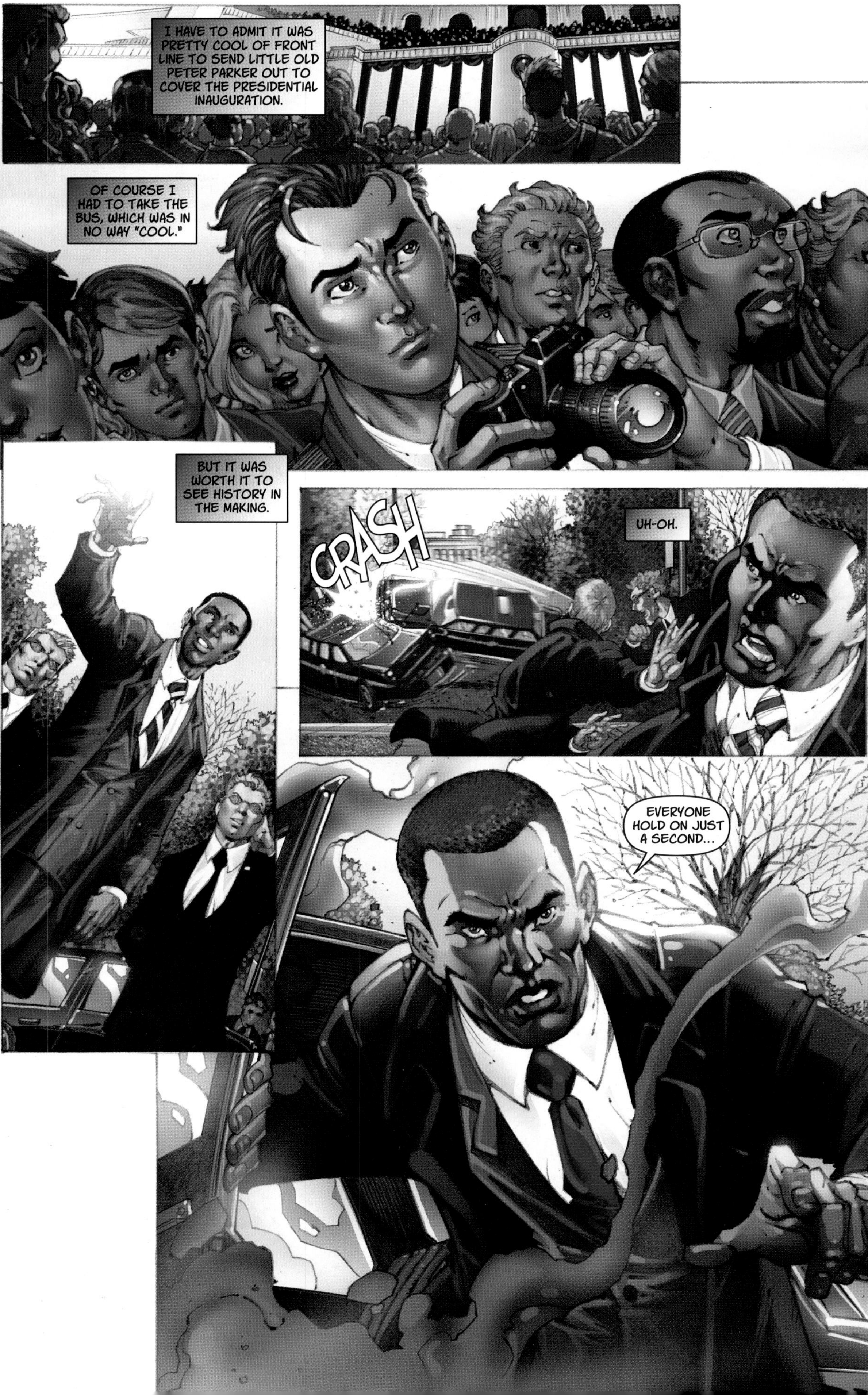
I HAVE TO ADMIT IT WAS PRETTY COOL OF FRONT LINE TO SEND LITTLE OLD PETER PARKER OUT TO COVER THE PRESIDENTIAL INAUGURATION.
OF COURSE I HAD TO TAKE THE BUS, WHICH WAS IN NO WAY "COOL."
BUT IT WAS WORTH IT TO SEE HISTORY IN THE MAKING.
CRASH
UH-OH.
EVERYONE HOLD ON JUST A SECOND...

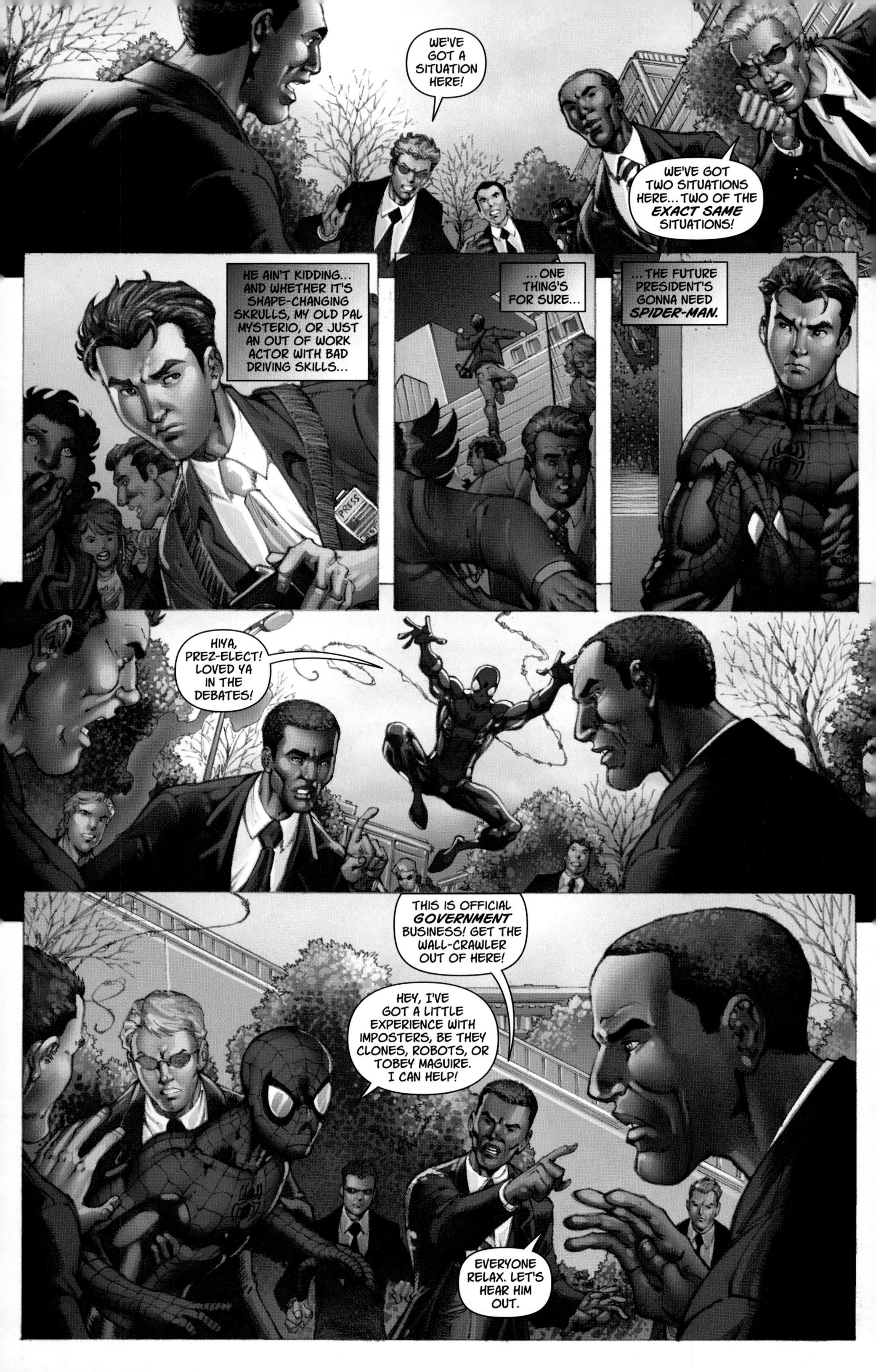
WE'VE GOT A SITUATION HERE!
WE'VE GOT TWO SITUATIONS HERE... TWO OF THE *EXACT SAME* SITUATIONS!
HE AIN'T KIDDING... AND WHETHER IT'S SHAPE-CHANGING SKRULLS, MY OLD PAL MYSTERIO, OR JUST AN OUT OF WORK ACTOR WITH BAD DRIVING SKILLS...
PRESS
...ONE THING'S FOR SURE...
...THE FUTURE PRESIDENT'S GONNA NEED *SPIDER-MAN.*
HIYA, PREZ-ELECT! LOVED YA IN THE DEBATES!
THIS IS OFFICIAL *GOVERNMENT* BUSINESS! GET THE WALL-CRAWLER OUT OF HERE!
HEY, I'VE GOT A LITTLE EXPERIENCE WITH IMPOSTERS, BE THEY CLONES, ROBOTS, OR TOBEY MAGUIRE. I CAN HELP!
EVERYONE RELAX. LET'S HEAR HIM OUT.

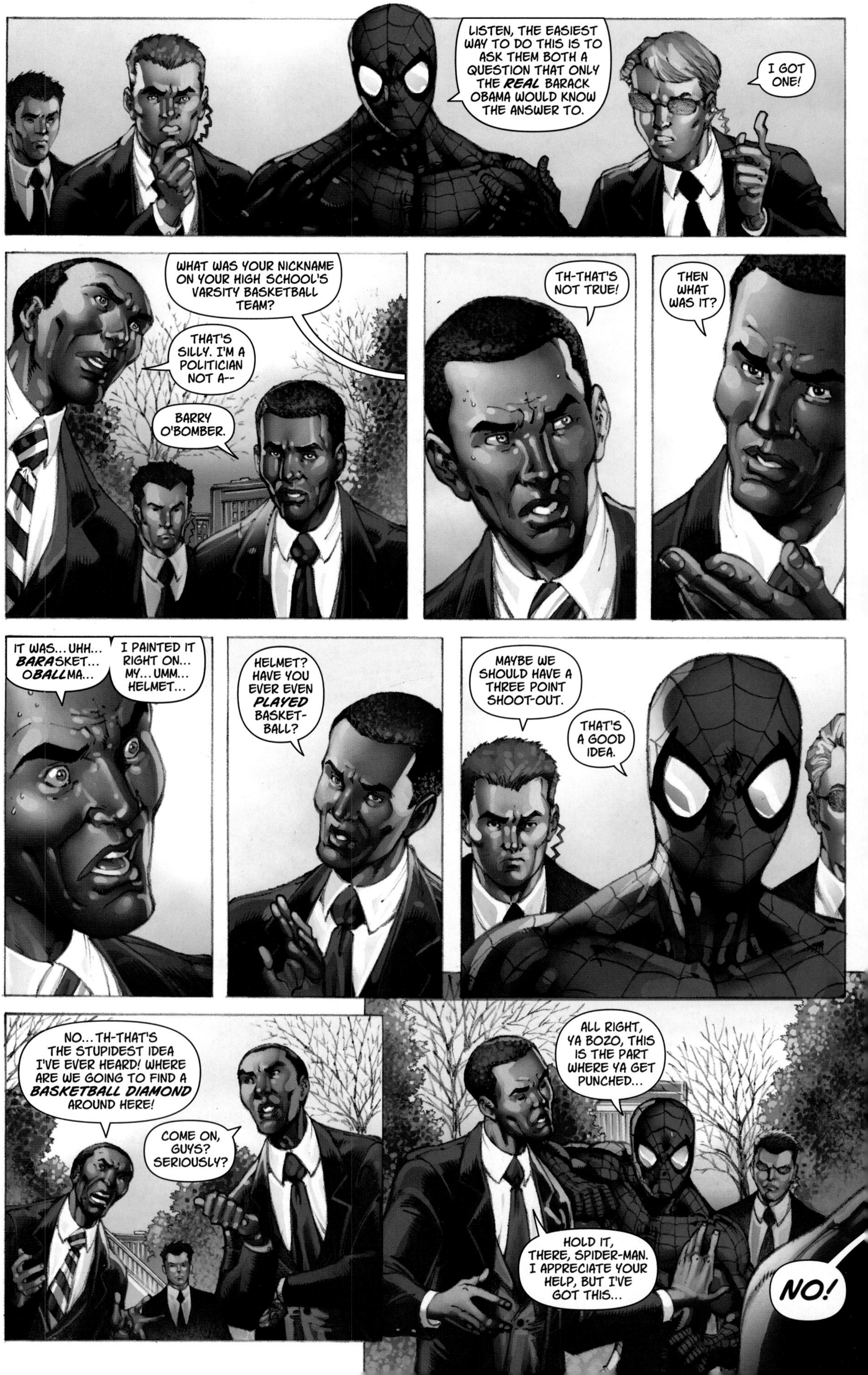
LISTEN, THE EASIEST WAY TO DO THIS IS TO ASK THEM BOTH A QUESTION THAT ONLY THE *REAL* BARACK OBAMA WOULD KNOW THE ANSWER TO.
I GOT ONE!
WHAT WAS YOUR NICKNAME ON YOUR HIGH SCHOOL'S VARSITY BASKETBALL TEAM?
THAT'S SILLY. I'M A POLITICIAN NOT A--
BARRY O'BOMBER.
TH-THAT'S NOT TRUE!
THEN WHAT WAS IT?
IT WAS... UHH... *BARA*SKET... *OBALL*MA...
I PAINTED IT RIGHT ON... MY... UMM... HELMET...
HELMET? HAVE YOU EVER EVEN *PLAYED* BASKET-BALL?
MAYBE WE SHOULD HAVE A THREE POINT SHOOT-OUT.
THAT'S A GOOD IDEA.
NO... TH-THAT'S THE STUPIDEST IDEA I'VE EVER HEARD! WHERE ARE WE GOING TO FIND A *BASKETBALL DIAMOND* AROUND HERE!
COME ON, GUYS? SERIOUSLY?
ALL RIGHT, YA BOZO, THIS IS THE PART WHERE YA GET PUNCHED...
HOLD IT, THERE, SPIDER-MAN. I APPRECIATE YOUR HELP, BUT I'VE GOT THIS...
NO!

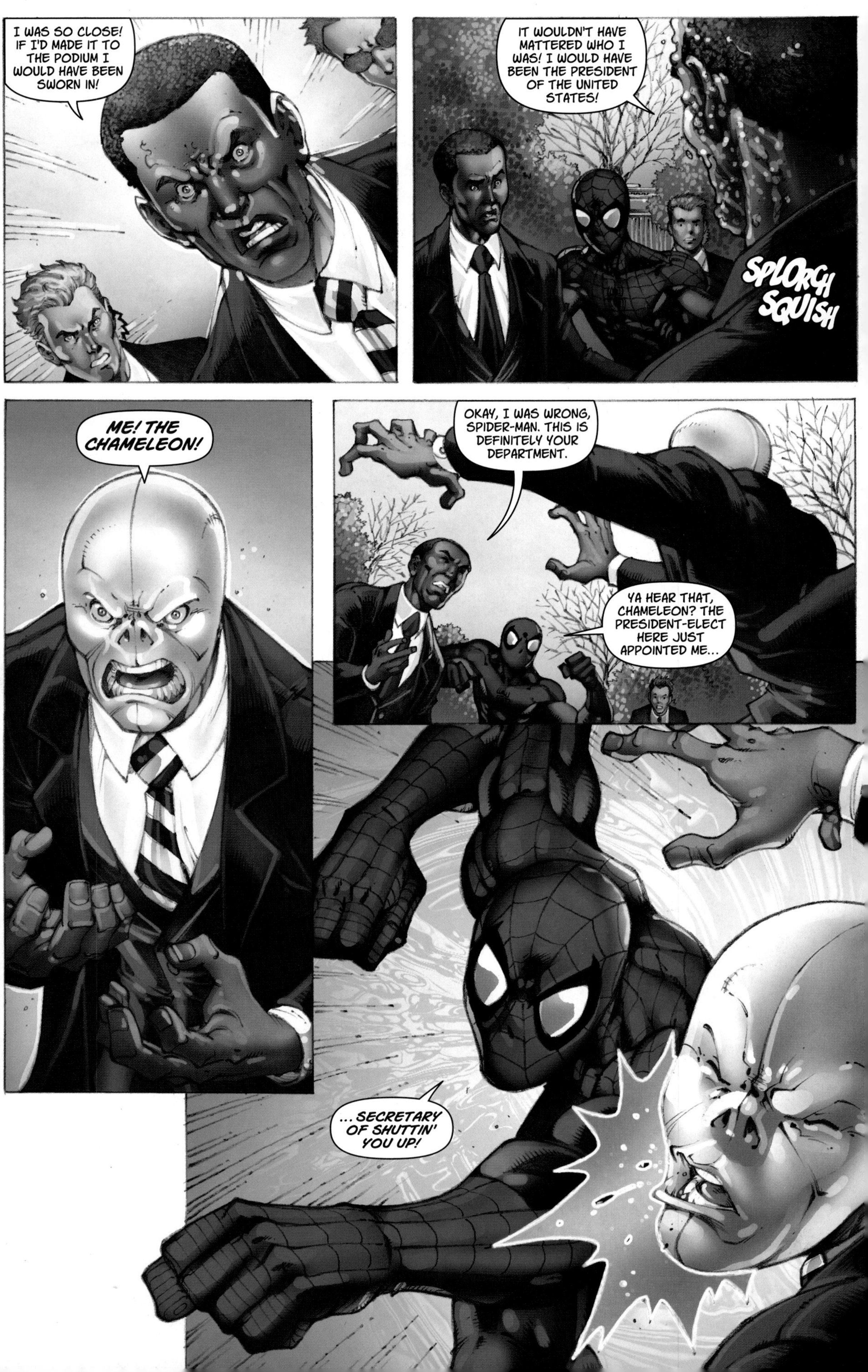
I WAS SO CLOSE! IF I'D MADE IT TO THE PODIUM I WOULD HAVE BEEN SWORN IN!
IT WOULDN'T HAVE MATTERED WHO I WAS! I WOULD HAVE BEEN THE PRESIDENT OF THE UNITED STATES!
SPLORCH SQUISH
ME! THE CHAMELEON!
OKAY, I WAS WRONG, SPIDER-MAN. THIS IS DEFINITELY YOUR DEPARTMENT.
YA HEAR THAT, CHAMELEON? THE PRESIDENT-ELECT HERE JUST APPOINTED ME...
...SECRETARY OF SHUTTIN' YOU UP!

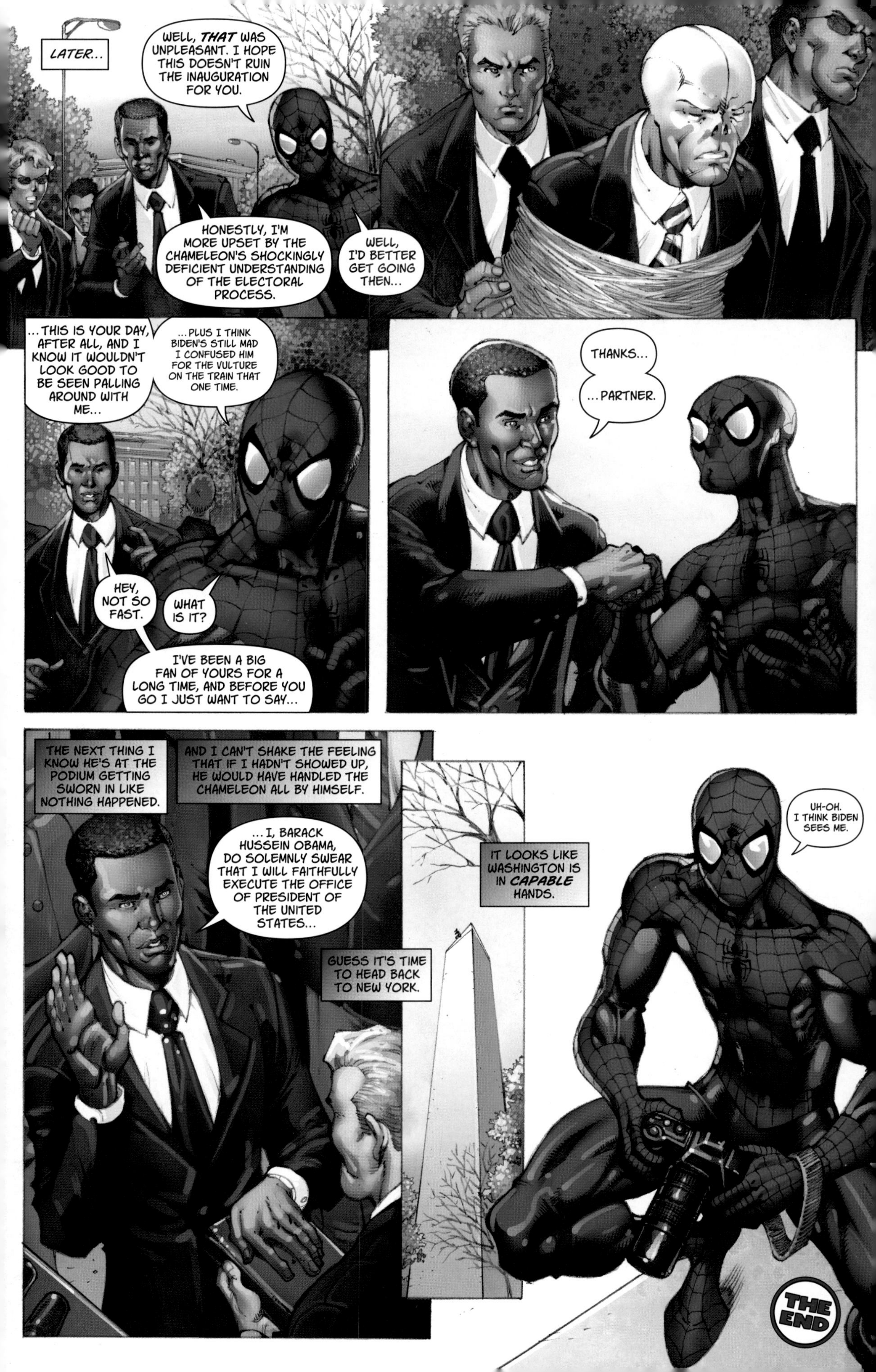
LATER...
WELL, THAT WAS UNPLEASANT. I HOPE THIS DOESN'T RUIN THE INAUGURATION FOR YOU.
HONESTLY, I'M MORE UPSET BY THE CHAMELEON'S SHOCKINGLY DEFICIENT UNDERSTANDING OF THE ELECTORAL PROCESS.
WELL, I'D BETTER GET GOING THEN...
...THIS IS YOUR DAY, AFTER ALL, AND I KNOW IT WOULDN'T LOOK GOOD TO BE SEEN PALLING AROUND WITH ME...
...PLUS I THINK BIDEN'S STILL MAD I CONFUSED HIM FOR THE VULTURE ON THE TRAIN THAT ONE TIME.
HEY, NOT SO FAST.
WHAT IS IT?
I'VE BEEN A BIG FAN OF YOURS FOR A LONG TIME, AND BEFORE YOU GO I JUST WANT TO SAY...
THANKS...
...PARTNER.
THE NEXT THING I KNOW HE'S AT THE PODIUM GETTING SWORN IN LIKE NOTHING HAPPENED.
AND I CAN'T SHAKE THE FEELING THAT IF I HADN'T SHOWED UP, HE WOULD HAVE HANDLED THE CHAMELEON ALL BY HIMSELF.
...I, BARACK HUSSEIN OBAMA, DO SOLEMNLY SWEAR THAT I WILL FAITHFULLY EXECUTE THE OFFICE OF PRESIDENT OF THE UNITED STATES...
GUESS IT'S TIME TO HEAD BACK TO NEW YORK.
IT LOOKS LIKE WASHINGTON IS IN CAPABLE HANDS.
UH-OH. I THINK BIDEN SEES ME.
THE END

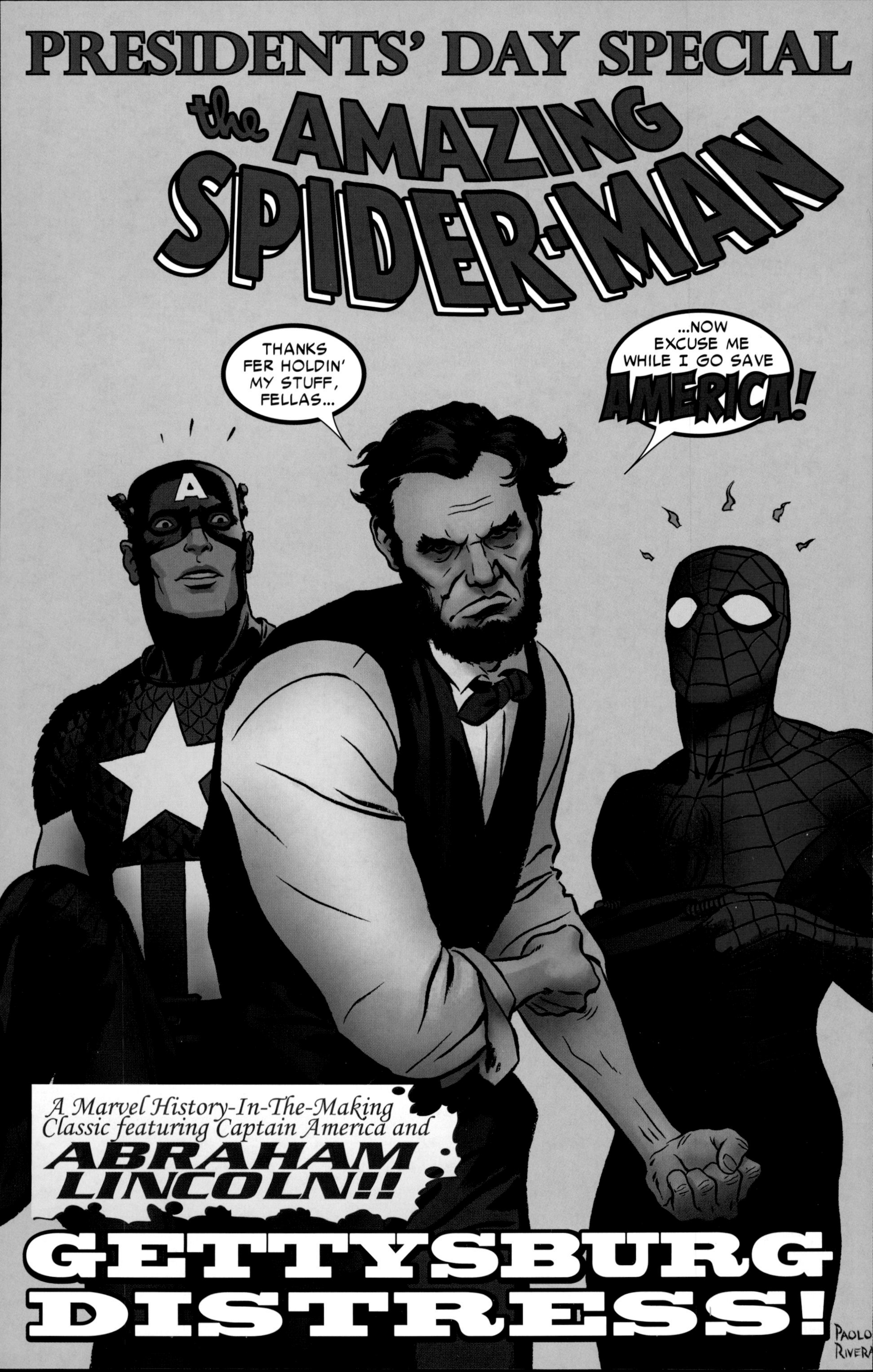
PRESIDENTS' DAY SPECIAL
the AMAZING SPIDER-MAN
THANKS FER HOLDIN' MY STUFF, FELLAS...
...NOW EXCUSE ME WHILE I GO SAVE AMERICA!
A Marvel History-In-The-Making Classic featuring Captain America and ABRAHAM LINCOLN!!
GETTYSBURG DISTRESS!
PAOLO RIVERA

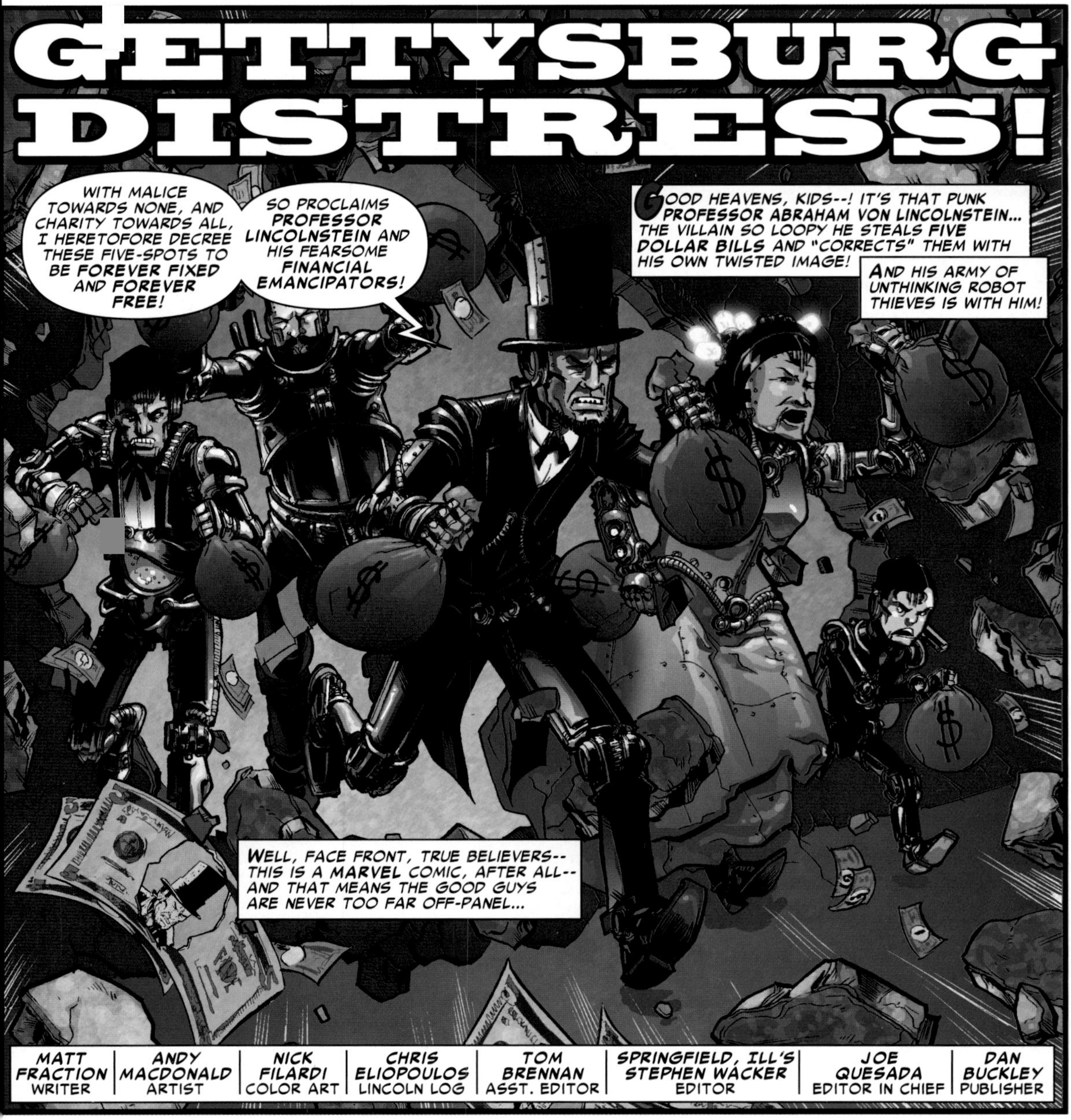
GETTYSBURG DISTRESS!
WITH MALICE TOWARDS NONE, AND CHARITY TOWARDS ALL, I HERETOFORE DECREE THESE FIVE-SPOTS TO BE FOREVER FIXED AND FOREVER FREE!
SO PROCLAIMS PROFESSOR LINCOLNSTEIN AND HIS FEARSOME FINANCIAL EMANCIPATORS!
GOOD HEAVENS, KIDS--! IT'S THAT PUNK PROFESSOR ABRAHAM VON LINCOLNSTEIN... THE VILLAIN SO LOOPY HE STEALS FIVE DOLLAR BILLS AND "CORRECTS" THEM WITH HIS OWN TWISTED IMAGE!
AND HIS ARMY OF UNTHINKING ROBOT THIEVES IS WITH HIM!
WELL, FACE FRONT, TRUE BELIEVERS--THIS IS A MARVEL COMIC, AFTER ALL--AND THAT MEANS THE GOOD GUYS ARE NEVER TOO FAR OFF-PANEL...
MATT FRACTION WRITER
ANDY MACDONALD ARTIST
NICK FILARDI COLOR ART
CHRIS ELIOPOULOS LINCOLN LOG
TOM BRENNAN ASST. EDITOR
SPRINGFIELD, ILL'S STEPHEN WACKER EDITOR
JOE QUESADA EDITOR IN CHIEF
DAN BUCKLEY PUBLISHER

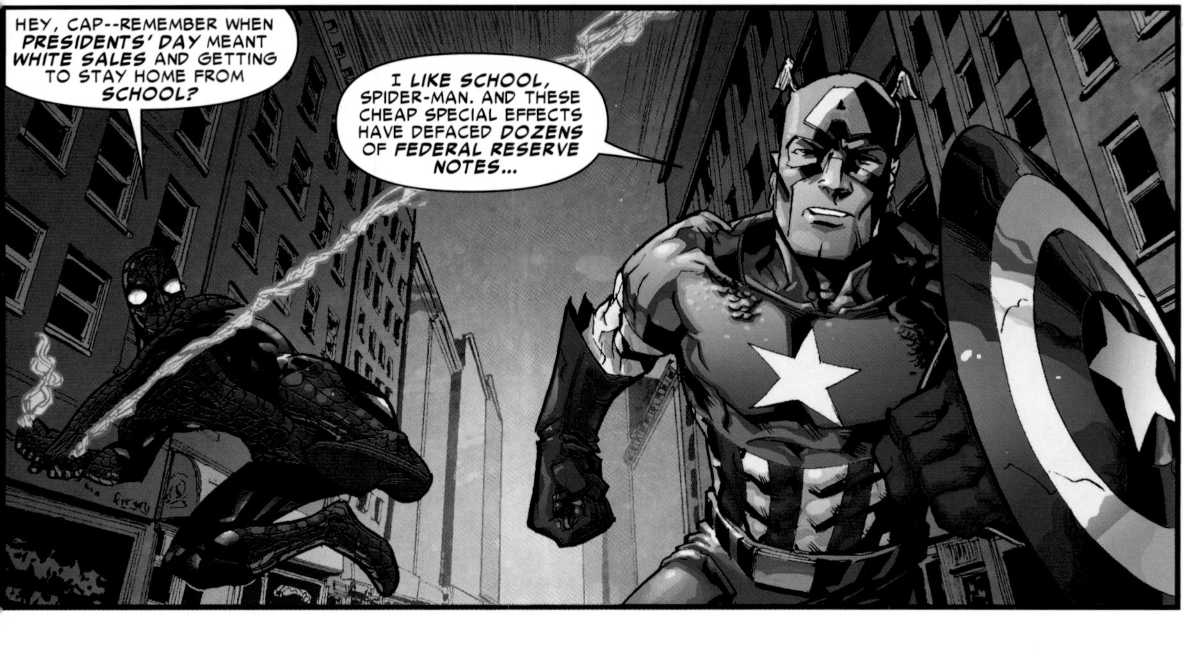
HEY, CAP--REMEMBER WHEN PRESIDENTS' DAY MEANT WHITE SALES AND GETTING TO STAY HOME FROM SCHOOL?
I LIKE SCHOOL, SPIDER-MAN. AND THESE CHEAP SPECIAL EFFECTS HAVE DEFACED DOZENS OF FEDERAL RESERVE NOTES...

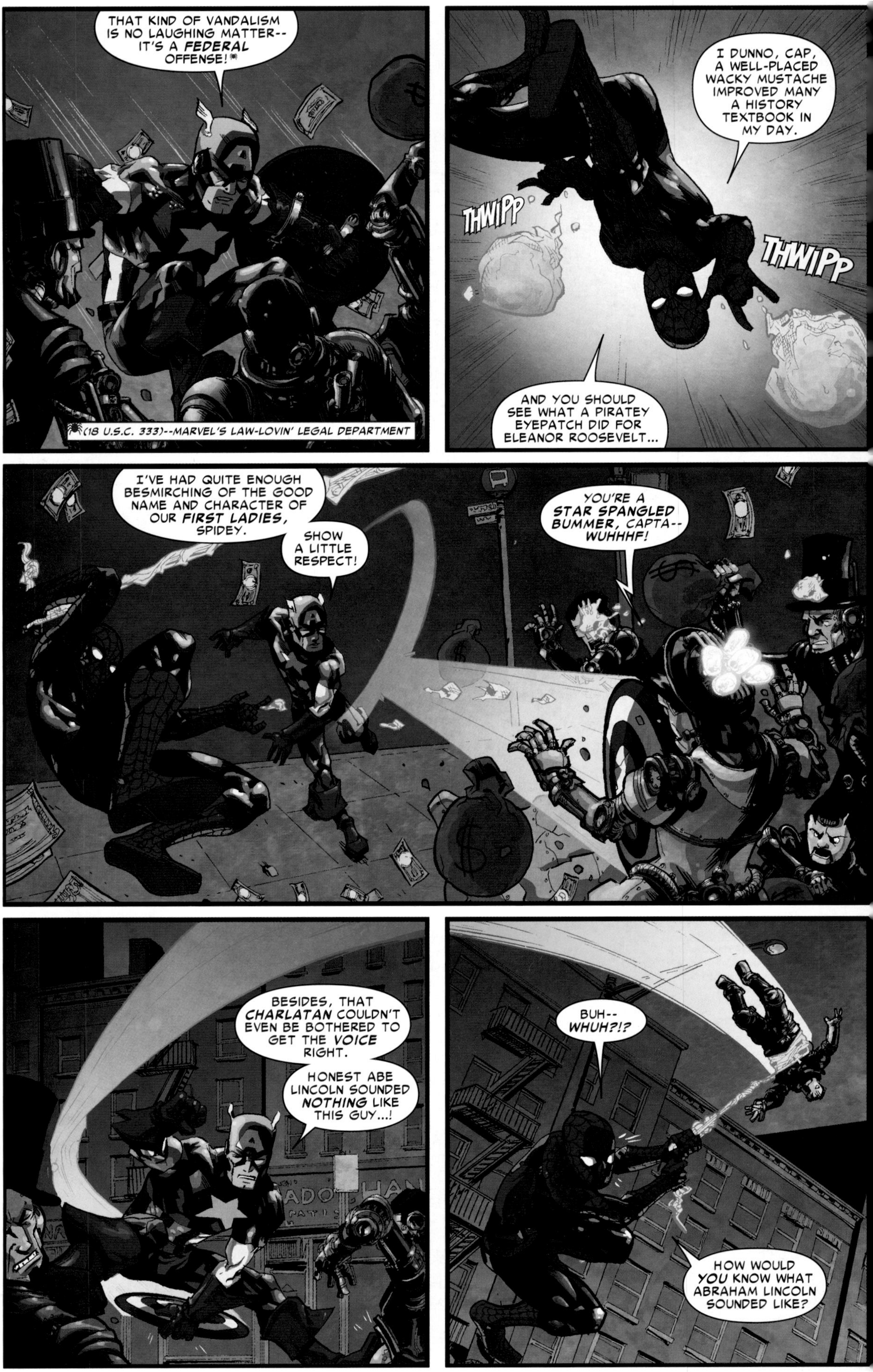
THAT KIND OF VANDALISM IS NO LAUGHING MATTER-- IT'S A FEDERAL OFFENSE!*
*(18 U.S.C. 333)--MARVEL'S LAW-LOVIN' LEGAL DEPARTMENT
I DUNNO, CAP, A WELL-PLACED WACKY MUSTACHE IMPROVED MANY A HISTORY TEXTBOOK IN MY DAY.
THWIPP
THWIPP
AND YOU SHOULD SEE WHAT A PIRATEY EYEPATCH DID FOR ELEANOR ROOSEVELT...
I'VE HAD QUITE ENOUGH BESMIRCHING OF THE GOOD NAME AND CHARACTER OF OUR FIRST LADIES, SPIDEY.
SHOW A LITTLE RESPECT!
YOU'RE A STAR SPANGLED BUMMER, CAPTA-- WUHHHF!
BESIDES, THAT CHARLATAN COULDN'T EVEN BE BOTHERED TO GET THE VOICE RIGHT.
HONEST ABE LINCOLN SOUNDED NOTHING LIKE THIS GUY...!
BUH-- WHUH?!?
HOW WOULD YOU KNOW WHAT ABRAHAM LINCOLN SOUNDED LIKE?

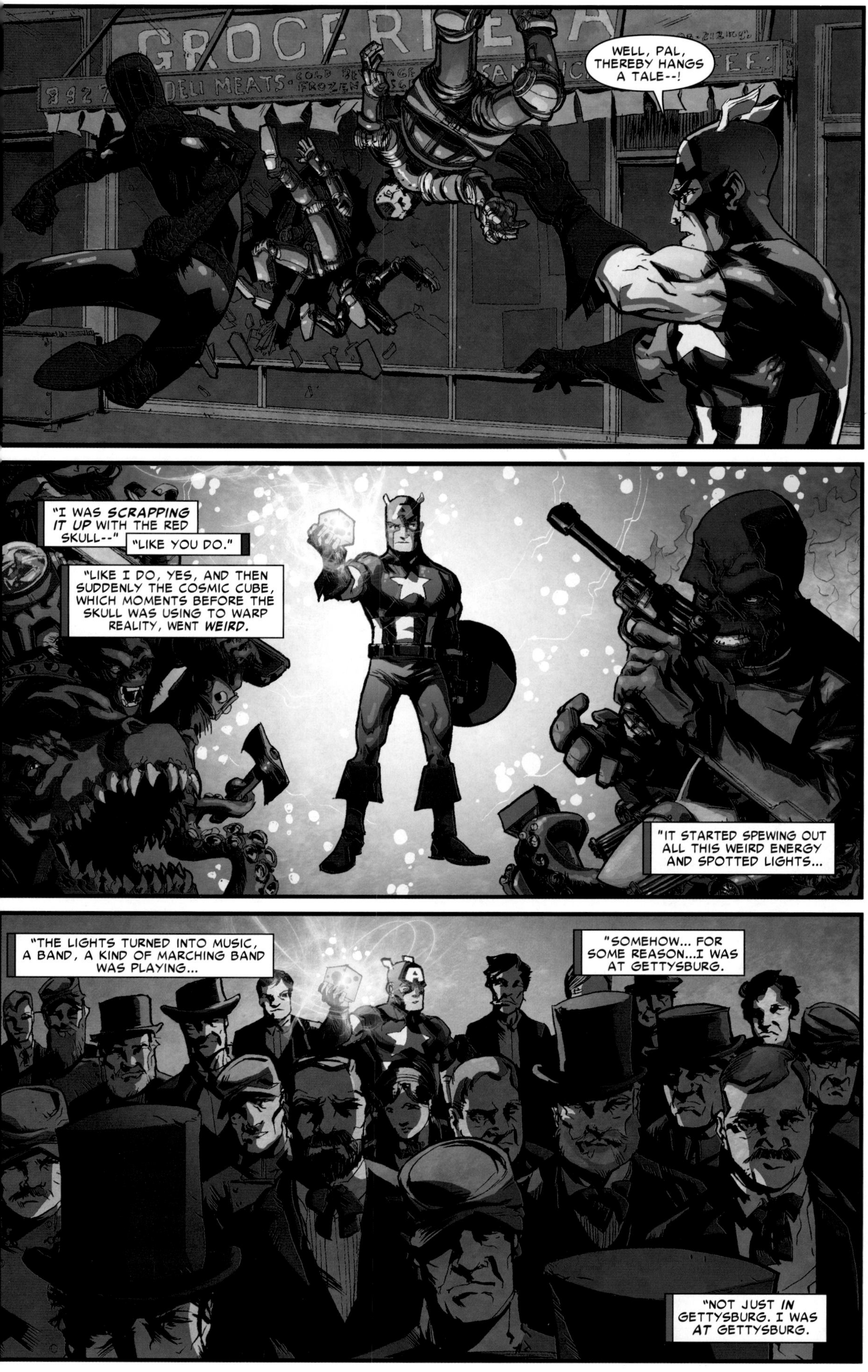
DELI MEATS
WELL, PAL, THEREBY HANGS A TALE--!
"I WAS *SCRAPPING IT UP* WITH THE RED SKULL--"
"LIKE YOU DO."
"LIKE I DO, YES, AND THEN SUDDENLY THE COSMIC CUBE, WHICH MOMENTS BEFORE THE SKULL WAS USING TO WARP REALITY, WENT *WEIRD*.
"IT STARTED SPEWING OUT ALL THIS WEIRD ENERGY AND SPOTTED LIGHTS...
"THE LIGHTS TURNED INTO MUSIC, A BAND, A KIND OF MARCHING BAND WAS PLAYING...
"SOMEHOW... FOR SOME REASON...I WAS AT GETTYSBURG.
"NOT JUST *IN* GETTYSBURG. I WAS *AT* GETTYSBURG.

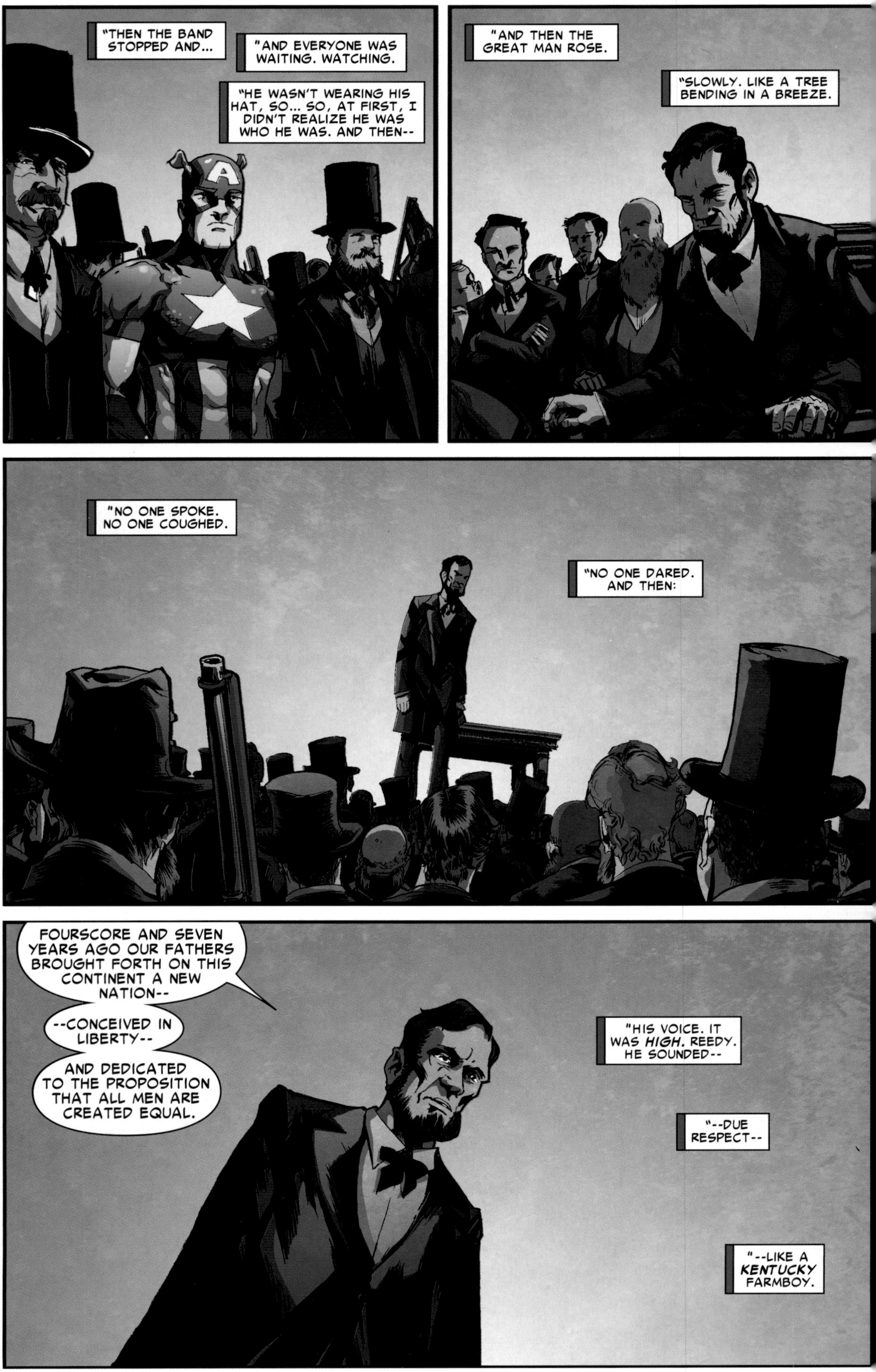

"THEN THE BAND STOPPED AND...
"AND EVERYONE WAS WAITING. WATCHING.
"HE WASN'T WEARING HIS HAT, SO... SO, AT FIRST, I DIDN'T REALIZE HE WAS WHO HE WAS. AND THEN--
"AND THEN THE GREAT MAN ROSE.
"SLOWLY. LIKE A TREE BENDING IN A BREEZE.
"NO ONE SPOKE. NO ONE COUGHED.
"NO ONE DARED. AND THEN:
FOURSCORE AND SEVEN YEARS AGO OUR FATHERS BROUGHT FORTH ON THIS CONTINENT A NEW NATION--
--CONCEIVED IN LIBERTY--
AND DEDICATED TO THE PROPOSITION THAT ALL MEN ARE CREATED EQUAL.
"HIS VOICE. IT WAS *HIGH*. REEDY. HE SOUNDED--
"--DUE RESPECT--
"--LIKE A *KENTUCKY* FARMBOY.

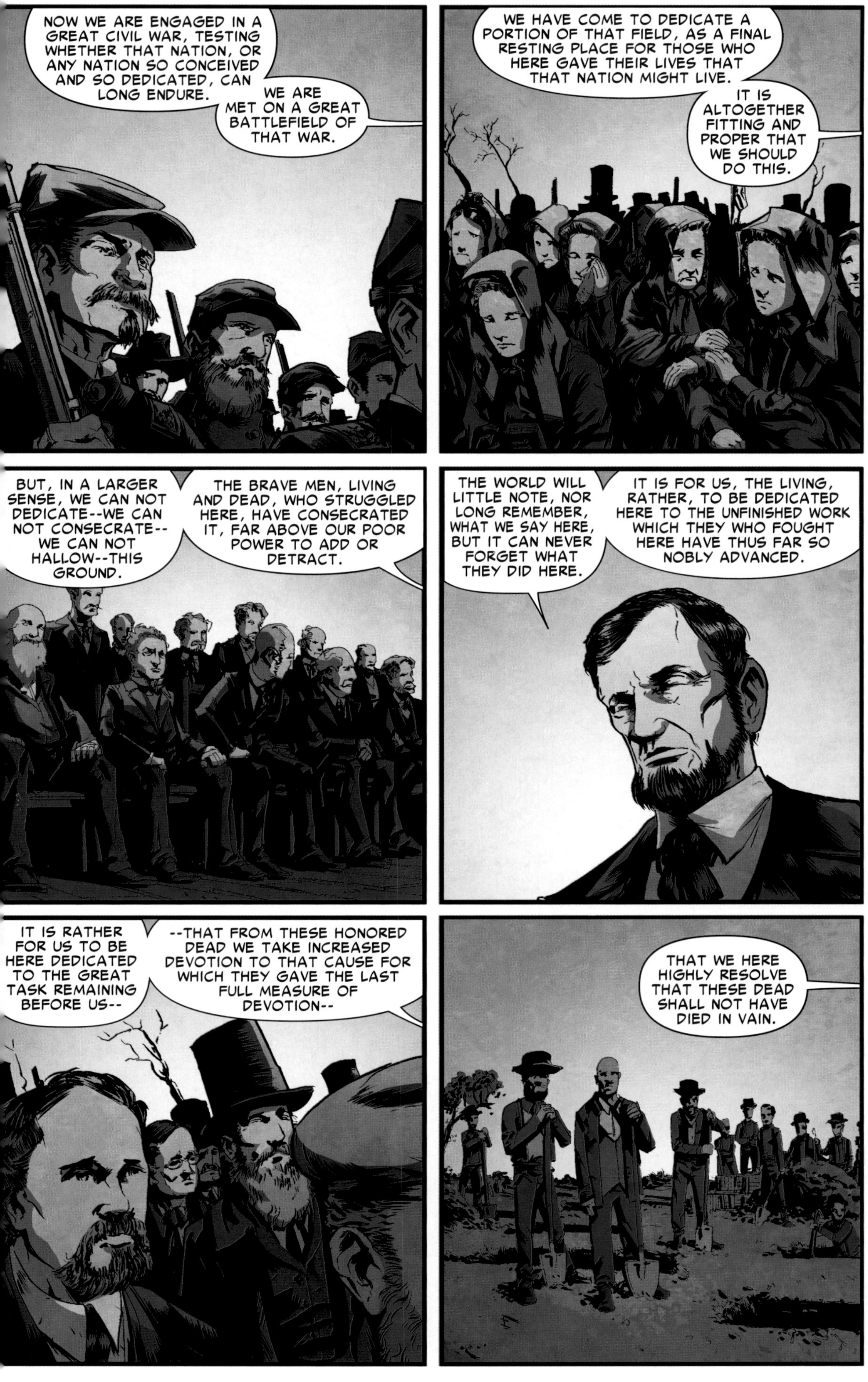
NOW WE ARE ENGAGED IN A GREAT CIVIL WAR, TESTING WHETHER THAT NATION, OR ANY NATION SO CONCEIVED AND SO DEDICATED, CAN LONG ENDURE.
WE ARE MET ON A GREAT BATTLEFIELD OF THAT WAR.
WE HAVE COME TO DEDICATE A PORTION OF THAT FIELD, AS A FINAL RESTING PLACE FOR THOSE WHO HERE GAVE THEIR LIVES THAT THAT NATION MIGHT LIVE.
IT IS ALTOGETHER FITTING AND PROPER THAT WE SHOULD DO THIS.
BUT, IN A LARGER SENSE, WE CAN NOT DEDICATE--WE CAN NOT CONSECRATE--WE CAN NOT HALLOW--THIS GROUND.
THE BRAVE MEN, LIVING AND DEAD, WHO STRUGGLED HERE, HAVE CONSECRATED IT, FAR ABOVE OUR POOR POWER TO ADD OR DETRACT.
THE WORLD WILL LITTLE NOTE, NOR LONG REMEMBER, WHAT WE SAY HERE, BUT IT CAN NEVER FORGET WHAT THEY DID HERE.
IT IS FOR US, THE LIVING, RATHER, TO BE DEDICATED HERE TO THE UNFINISHED WORK WHICH THEY WHO FOUGHT HERE HAVE THUS FAR SO NOBLY ADVANCED.
IT IS RATHER FOR US TO BE HERE DEDICATED TO THE GREAT TASK REMAINING BEFORE US--
--THAT FROM THESE HONORED DEAD WE TAKE INCREASED DEVOTION TO THAT CAUSE FOR WHICH THEY GAVE THE LAST FULL MEASURE OF DEVOTION--
THAT WE HERE HIGHLY RESOLVE THAT THESE DEAD SHALL NOT HAVE DIED IN VAIN.

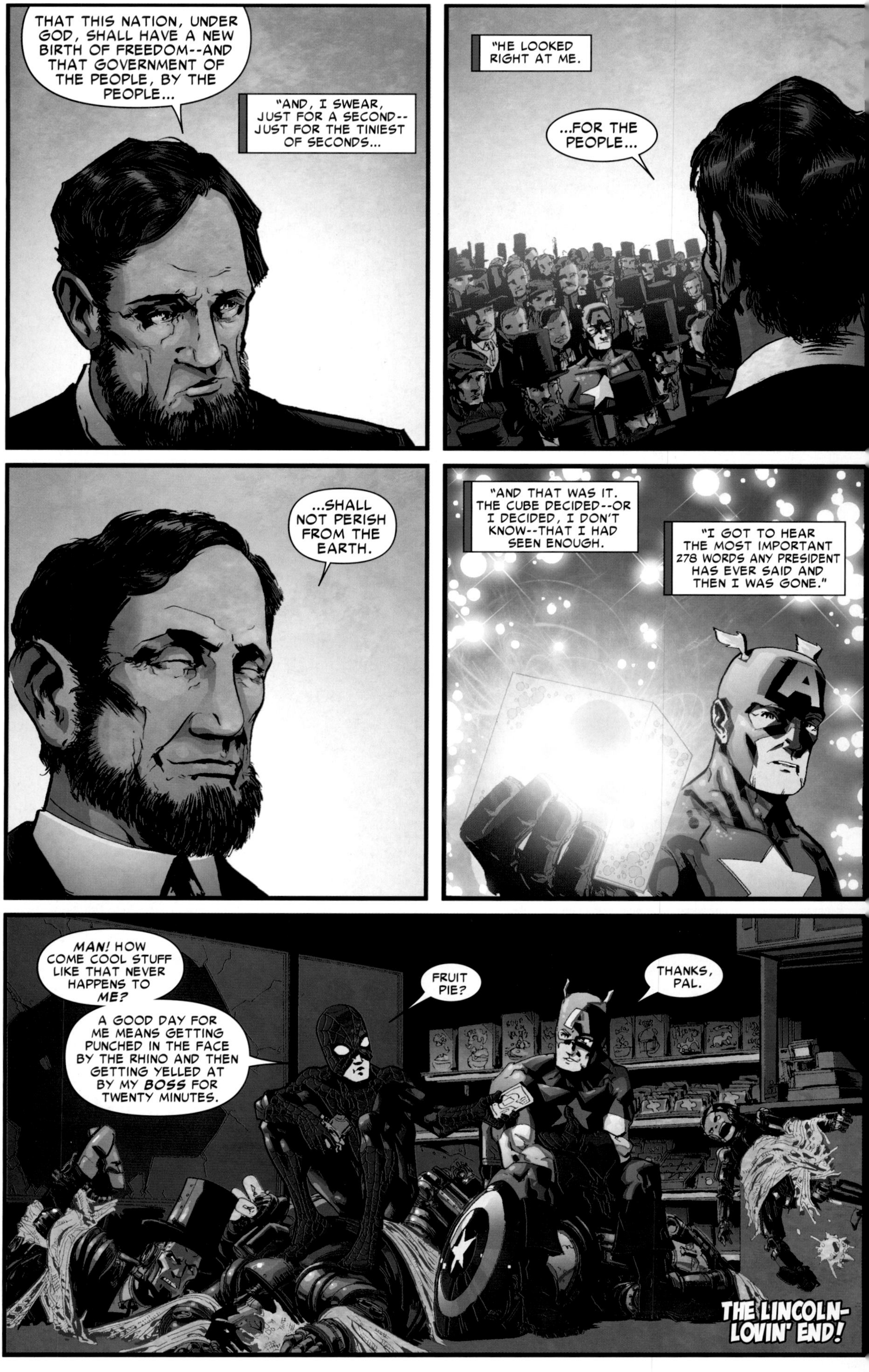
THAT THIS NATION, UNDER GOD, SHALL HAVE A NEW BIRTH OF FREEDOM--AND THAT GOVERNMENT OF THE PEOPLE, BY THE PEOPLE...
"AND, I SWEAR, JUST FOR A SECOND-- JUST FOR THE TINIEST OF SECONDS...
"HE LOOKED RIGHT AT ME.
...FOR THE PEOPLE...
...SHALL NOT PERISH FROM THE EARTH.
"AND THAT WAS IT. THE CUBE DECIDED--OR I DECIDED, I DON'T KNOW--THAT I HAD SEEN ENOUGH.
"I GOT TO HEAR THE MOST IMPORTANT 278 WORDS ANY PRESIDENT HAS EVER SAID AND THEN I WAS GONE."
MAN! HOW COME COOL STUFF LIKE THAT NEVER HAPPENS TO ME?
A GOOD DAY FOR ME MEANS GETTING PUNCHED IN THE FACE BY THE RHINO AND THEN GETTING YELLED AT BY MY BOSS FOR TWENTY MINUTES.
FRUIT PIE?
THANKS, PAL.
THE LINCOLN-LOVIN' END!

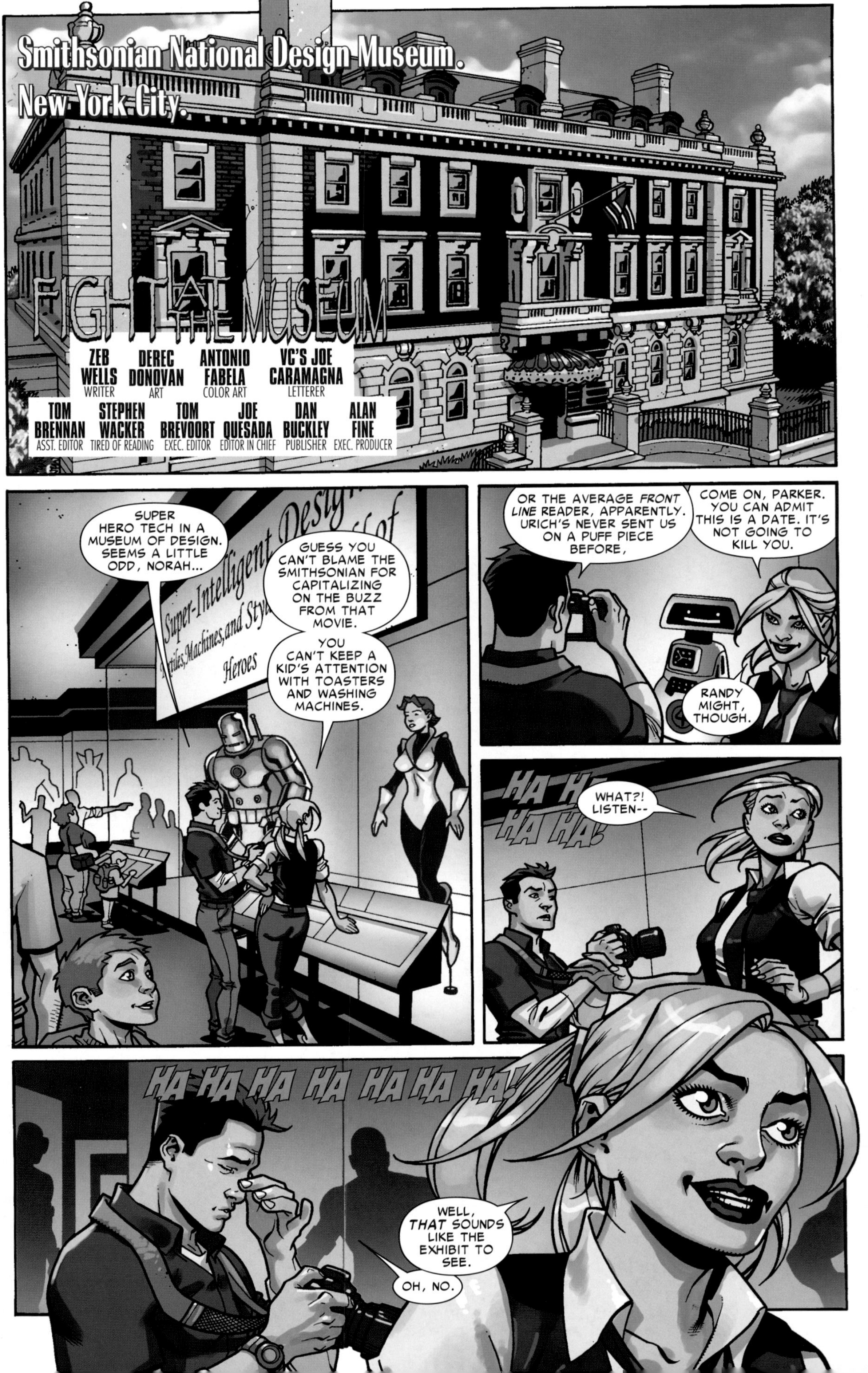
Smithsonian National Design Museum.
New York City.
FIGHT AT THE MUSEUM
ZEB WELLS WRITER
DEREC DONOVAN ART
ANTONIO FABELA COLOR ART
VC'S JOE CARAMAGNA LETTERER
TOM BRENNAN ASST. EDITOR
STEPHEN WACKER TIRED OF READING
TOM BREVOORT EXEC. EDITOR
JOE QUESADA EDITOR IN CHIEF
DAN BUCKLEY PUBLISHER
ALAN FINE EXEC. PRODUCER
Super-Intelligent Design
Textiles, Machines, and Style of Heroes
SUPER HERO TECH IN A MUSEUM OF DESIGN. SEEMS A LITTLE ODD, NORAH...
GUESS YOU CAN'T BLAME THE SMITHSONIAN FOR CAPITALIZING ON THE BUZZ FROM THAT MOVIE.
YOU CAN'T KEEP A KID'S ATTENTION WITH TOASTERS AND WASHING MACHINES.
OR THE AVERAGE *FRONT LINE* READER, APPARENTLY. URICH'S NEVER SENT US ON A PUFF PIECE BEFORE.
COME ON, PARKER. YOU CAN ADMIT THIS IS A DATE. IT'S NOT GOING TO KILL YOU.
RANDY MIGHT, THOUGH.
HA HA HA HA!
WHAT?! LISTEN--
HA HA HA HA HA HA HA!
WELL, *THAT* SOUNDS LIKE THE EXHIBIT TO SEE.
OH, NO.

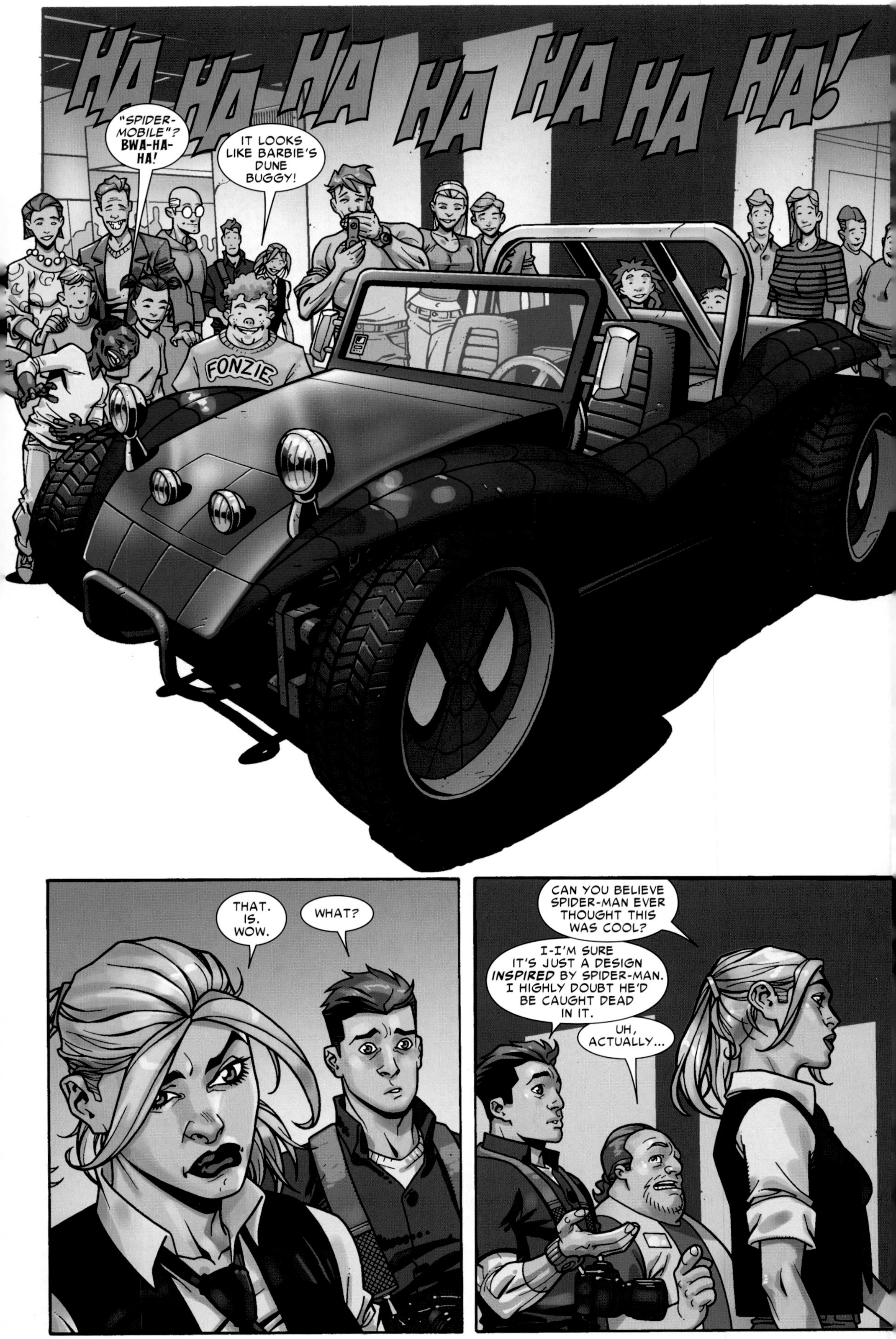
HA HA HA HA HA HA HA!
"SPIDER-MOBILE"? BWA-HA-HA!
IT LOOKS LIKE BARBIE'S DUNE BUGGY!
FONZIE
THAT. IS. WOW.
WHAT?
CAN YOU BELIEVE SPIDER-MAN EVER THOUGHT THIS WAS COOL?
I-I'M SURE IT'S JUST A DESIGN *INSPIRED* BY SPIDER-MAN. I HIGHLY DOUBT HE'D BE CAUGHT DEAD IN IT.
UH, ACTUALLY...

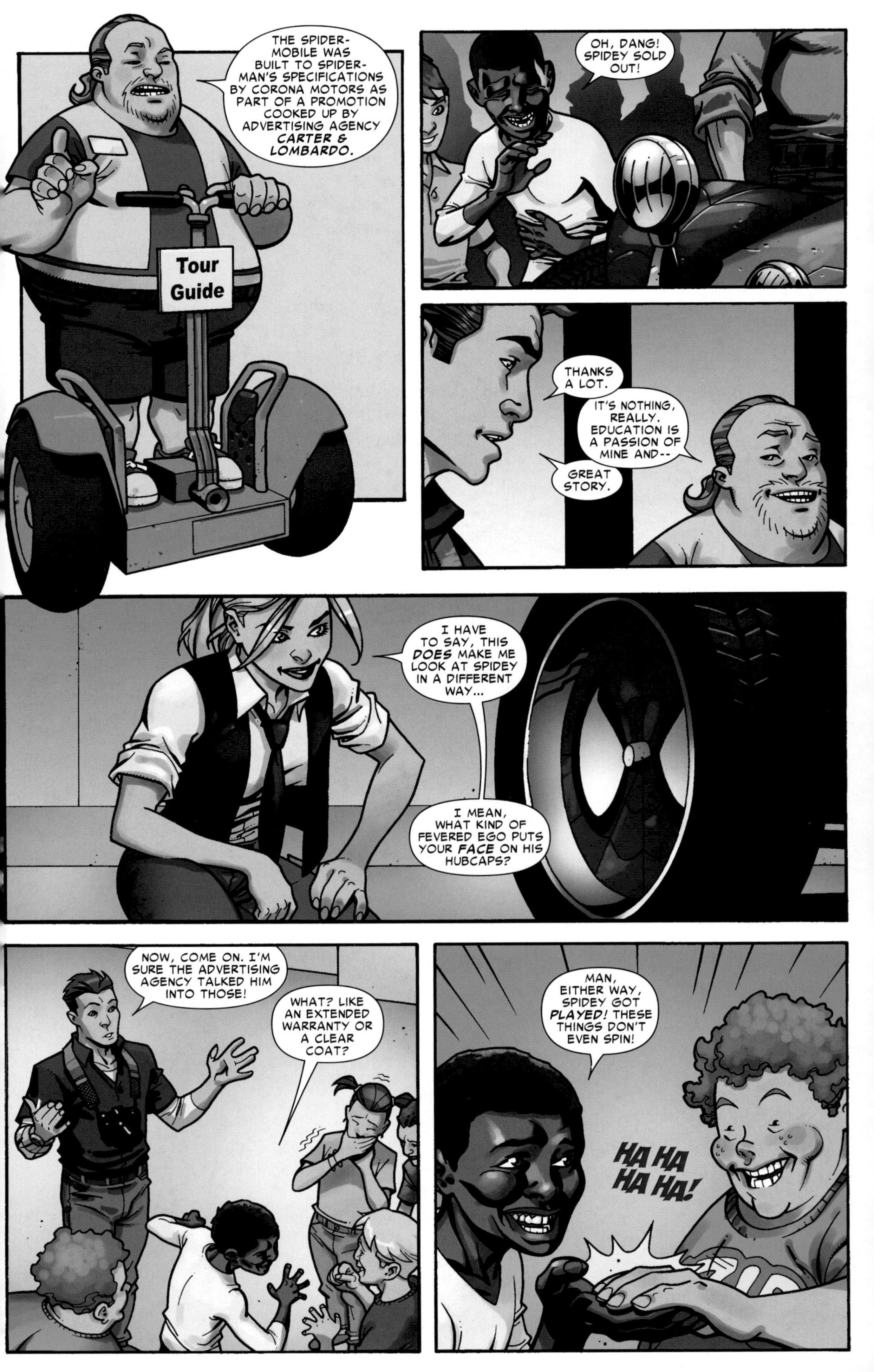
THE SPIDER-MOBILE WAS BUILT TO SPIDER-MAN'S SPECIFICATIONS BY CORONA MOTORS AS PART OF A PROMOTION COOKED UP BY ADVERTISING AGENCY CARTER & LOMBARDO.
Tour Guide
OH, DANG! SPIDEY SOLD OUT!
THANKS A LOT.
IT'S NOTHING, REALLY. EDUCATION IS A PASSION OF MINE AND--
GREAT STORY.
I HAVE TO SAY, THIS DOES MAKE ME LOOK AT SPIDEY IN A DIFFERENT WAY...
I MEAN, WHAT KIND OF FEVERED EGO PUTS YOUR FACE ON HIS HUBCAPS?
NOW, COME ON. I'M SURE THE ADVERTISING AGENCY TALKED HIM INTO THOSE!
WHAT? LIKE AN EXTENDED WARRANTY OR A CLEAR COAT?
MAN, EITHER WAY, SPIDEY GOT PLAYED! THESE THINGS DON'T EVEN SPIN!
HA HA HA HA!

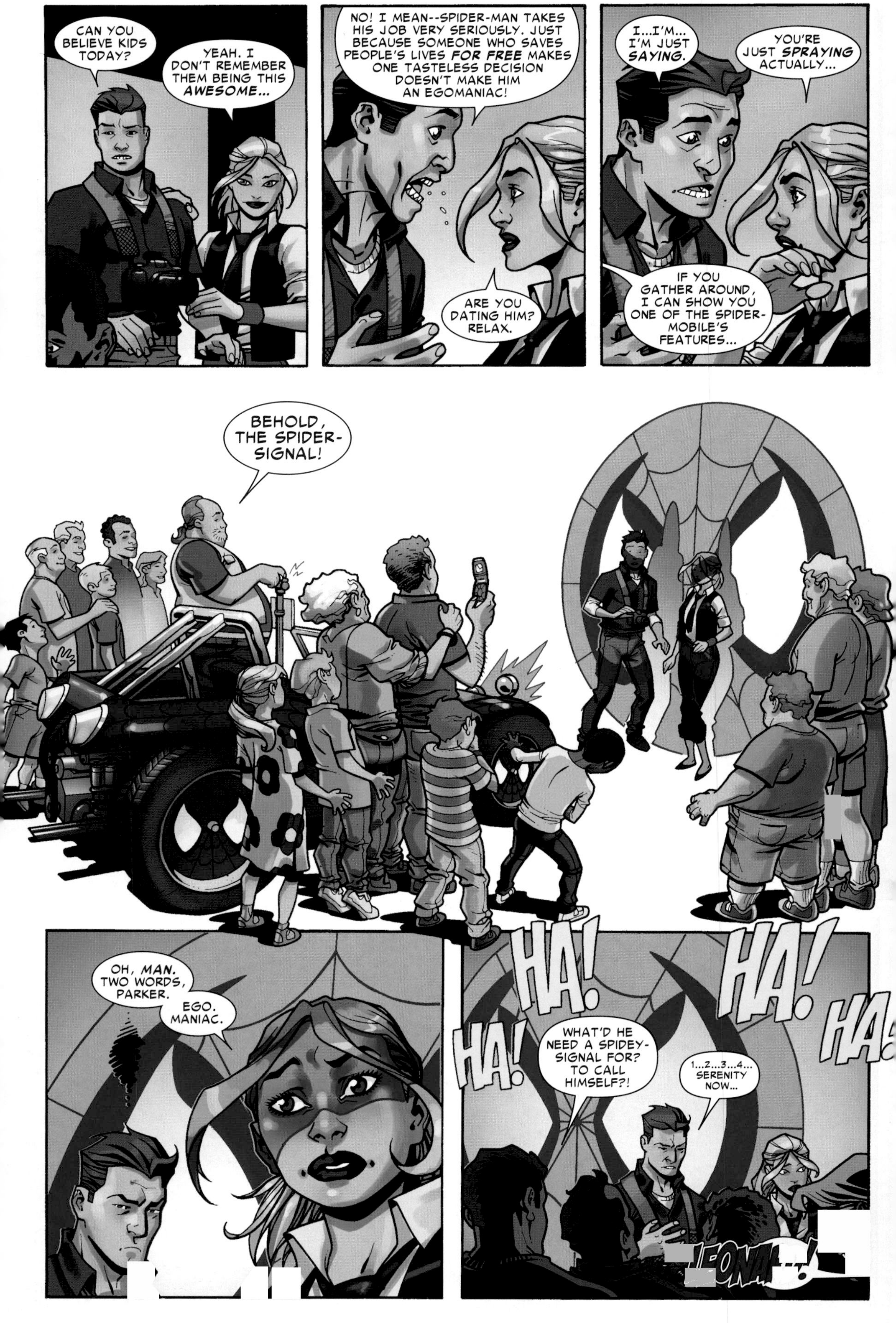
CAN YOU BELIEVE KIDS TODAY?
YEAH. I DON'T REMEMBER THEM BEING THIS AWESOME...
NO! I MEAN--SPIDER-MAN TAKES HIS JOB VERY SERIOUSLY. JUST BECAUSE SOMEONE WHO SAVES PEOPLE'S LIVES FOR FREE MAKES ONE TASTELESS DECISION DOESN'T MAKE HIM AN EGOMANIAC!
ARE YOU DATING HIM? RELAX.
I...I'M... I'M JUST SAYING.
YOU'RE JUST SPRAYING ACTUALLY...
IF YOU GATHER AROUND, I CAN SHOW YOU ONE OF THE SPIDER-MOBILE'S FEATURES...
BEHOLD, THE SPIDER-SIGNAL!
OH, MAN. TWO WORDS, PARKER.
EGO. MANIAC.
HA! HA! HA! HA!
WHAT'D HE NEED A SPIDEY-SIGNAL FOR? TO CALL HIMSELF?!
1...2...3...4... SERENITY NOW...

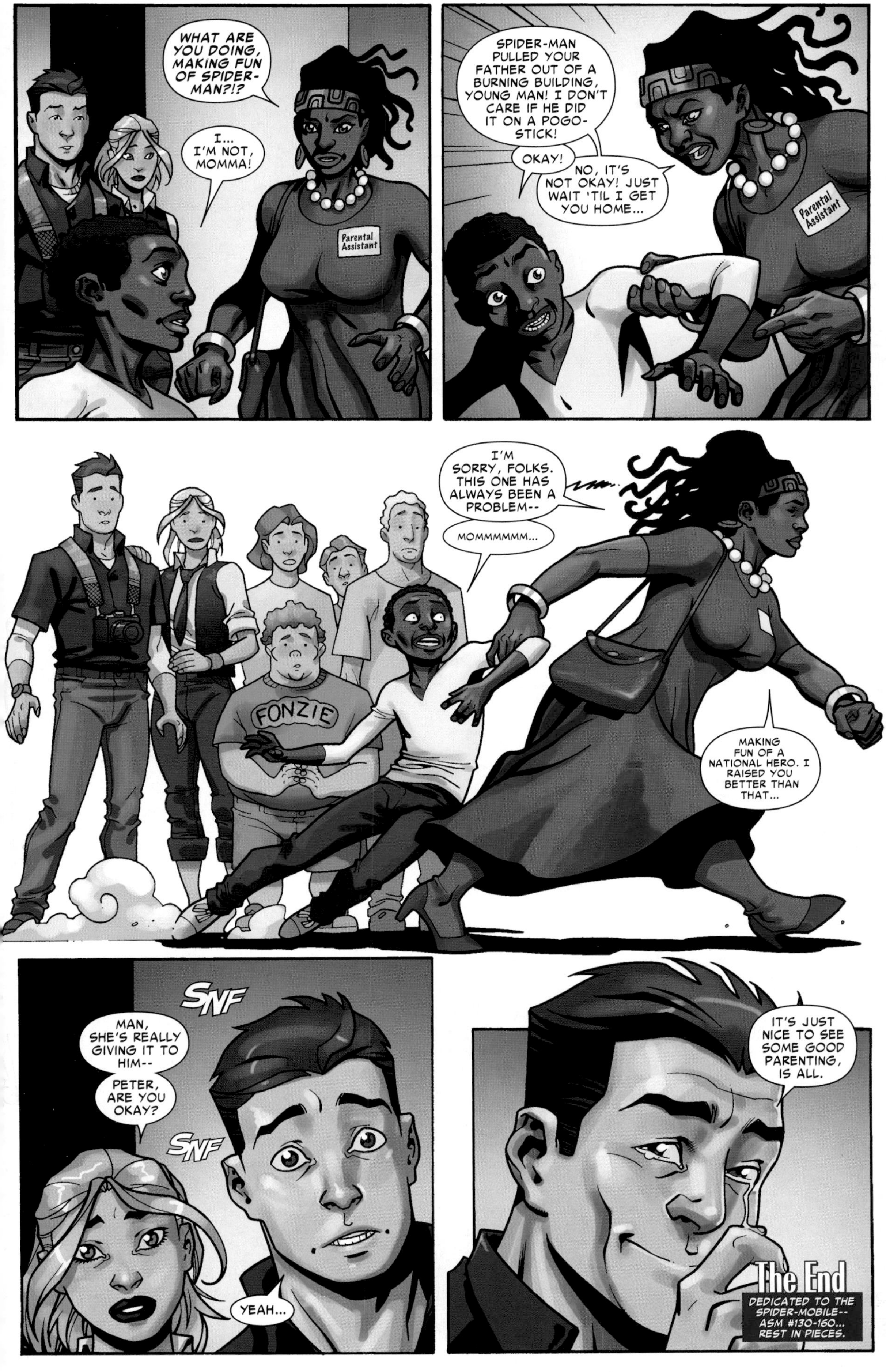
WHAT ARE YOU DOING, MAKING FUN OF SPIDER-MAN?!?
I... I'M NOT, MOMMA!
Parental Assistant
SPIDER-MAN PULLED YOUR FATHER OUT OF A BURNING BUILDING, YOUNG MAN! I DON'T CARE IF HE DID IT ON A POGO-STICK!
OKAY!
NO, IT'S NOT OKAY! JUST WAIT 'TIL I GET YOU HOME...
Parental Assistant
I'M SORRY, FOLKS. THIS ONE HAS ALWAYS BEEN A PROBLEM--
MOMMMMMM...
FONZIE
MAKING FUN OF A NATIONAL HERO. I RAISED YOU BETTER THAN THAT...
SNF
MAN, SHE'S REALLY GIVING IT TO HIM--
PETER, ARE YOU OKAY?
SNF
YEAH...
IT'S JUST NICE TO SEE SOME GOOD PARENTING, IS ALL.
The End
DEDICATED TO THE SPIDER-MOBILE-- ASM #130-160... REST IN PIECES.

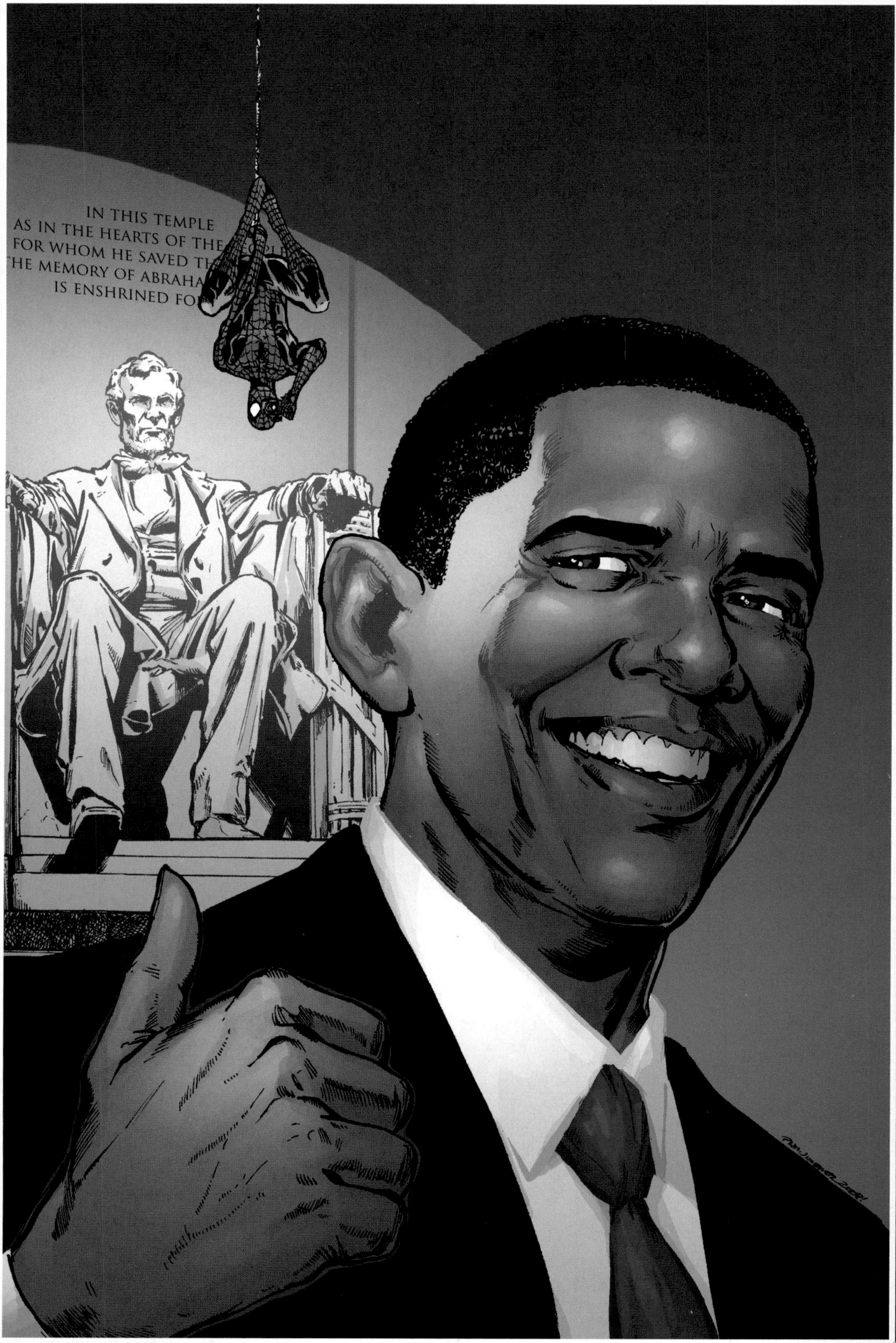
IN THIS TEMPLE
AS IN THE HEARTS OF THE
FOR WHOM HE SAVED TH
THE MEMORY OF ABRAHA
IS ENSHRINED FO